TENNEY

★ American Girl®

TENNEY

by **Kellen** Hertz

Scholastic Inc.

Cover illustration by Juliana Kolesova
Author photo credit, p. 181: Sonya Sones

ISBN 978-1-338-14883-1

10 9 8 7 6 5 4 3 2 1   17 18 19 20 21

Printed in the U.S.A. 23 • First printing 2017

★ ★

For John, who taught me how to listen,
and for Kieran, who dances to his own beat

CONTENTS

LOST IN THE MUSIC

Chapter 1

*M*y left hand shifted down the neck of my guitar, fingers pressing into the frets to form chords, while my right hand sailed over the strings with my favorite pick. I knew every note of "April Springs." I didn't have to look at my sheet music or think about how to play the song. I just let go and played, feeling the music as if it was flowing out of my heart.

Out of the corner of my eye, I caught Dad waving me down from a few feet away.

Startled, I clamped my hand over my guitar's neck, muting its sound mid-chord. It took me a moment to realize I didn't hear the buzzy twang of Dad's bass guitar. I glanced around. The rest of our band wasn't playing, either.

"Sorry," I said, feeling my cheeks turn hot pink.

"No worries," Dad said, winking. "I know you love that one. And you were singing with so much heart that it nearly broke mine to stop you."

I blushed. When I play a song I love, it's easy for me to get swept up and forget about everything but the music. "April Springs" has a slow, sad melody that fills me with warmth every time we rehearse it. And when I sing its romantic lyrics, I can't help daydreaming about what the songwriter must have been feeling when she composed them.

"That transition out of the chorus still sounds a bit rocky," Dad said to the band. "Let's try it again."

Our lead singer, Jesse, wrinkled her nose at him. "Come on, Ray. This is the fifth time we've gone over the chorus. Let's just move on to the next song."

My seventeen-year-old brother, Mason, rolled his eyes from behind his drum kit. Mason isn't Jesse's biggest fan. He thinks she's stuck-up because she never helps unpack gear at our shows. Also, she only drinks bottled water from France, even though the tap water is perfectly fine here in Nashville, Tennessee. Despite all that, I couldn't help but

admire her. Jesse definitely had what it took to be
a lead singer for a band. She had a great voice, she
loved performing, and she was happiest when she
was the center of attention. Every time I watched
her perform I wondered: *Could that be me someday?*

"Let's try the chorus *once* more," Dad replied
calmly. "We haven't practiced in ages. And with our
next show around the corner, I want to make sure
we have this down."

Jesse pouted, but she knew she couldn't say no
because the Tri-Stars were Dad's band.

The Tri-Stars used to be a family band. But
when Mom quit to start her own food truck business, Dad invited Jesse to join us as the lead singer.
I wish we got to perform at the big stages around
Nashville, like the Ryman Auditorium or the Grand
Ole Opry, but we mostly just play weekend gigs
around our neighborhood. Even so, we have a few
fans—that is, if you count my little sister and my
best friend.

Jesse sighed. "Let's get on with it, then." She
counted off, and the four of us launched into
"April Springs" again.

"Last April the rains came down," sang Jesse, *"and washed away your love."*

Dad and I joined in, harmonizing on the next lines. *"Last April the rains came down, and washed away my pride. When I lost your heart in that rainstorm, I think I nearly died."*

Jesse pushed her microphone away and looked over her shoulder at me.

"Tennyson, your vocals need to blend more," she hissed.

Jesse always uses my full name when she bosses me around. Usually I like having a unique name, but the way Jesse says it always makes my temper rise into my throat.

"I'm doing my best," I said to her.

I like singing harmony, but when I'm singing low notes, my voice loses some of its smoothness and gets a grainy edge. Mom says that's what makes my voice unique. When you're singing backup, though, you're not supposed to sound unique; you're supposed to sound *invisible*.

"It's boiling in here," Jesse said curtly. "I need a break." Without waiting for my dad's reaction, she stepped off the edge of the stage and slipped out the front door.

Dad frowned. "I'll go turn up the AC," he said, heading to the storeroom at the back of the shop where we rehearse.

I sighed. We never seemed to be able to get through an entire rehearsal without Jesse getting upset—and this time it was my fault.

Mason slung an arm around my shoulders. "Don't let Jesse get to you," he said. "She's not happy unless she's complaining about something. I thought you sounded great. Didn't she, Waylon?"

Waylon, our golden retriever, perked up. He's named after one of Dad's favorite singers, the "outlaw" Waylon Jennings, and he definitely lived up to the name when he was a puppy. He always used to break the rules, like escaping from the backyard and chewing up our shoes.

"Maybe the Tri-Stars should try playing some of your songs," Mason suggested, nudging me with his drumstick. "Remember that one you wrote about Waylon? *Oh, Waylon. Wayyy-lon! He's a real sweet pooch . . .*" he crooned.

I sang the next line. *"Long as you make sure he's not on the loose ... "*

"Wayyy-lon," we harmonized. Waylon howled along.

I laughed. "I don't think those lyrics are ready for an audience yet."

"C'mon, it's a good song!" Mason said.

"It's just okay," I said.

I'm twelve now, but I've been writing songs since I was ten. "Waylon's Song" was the first one I ever shared with my family. I was really proud of it back then. Now, though, the words seemed sort of cheesy.

"I've gotten better since I wrote that one," I said.

"Yeah?" Mason said. "You should play me something."

I hesitated. I'd been working on a few songs lately, but none of them were quite ready for anyone's ears but mine.

"I need to finish some lyrics first," I said.

"Suit yourself. Want to help me catch up on inventory while we wait for Jesse?"

We always hold Tri-Star rehearsals at my dad's

music shop, Grant's Music and Collectibles. My parents have owned the store since I was little, so for me, it's the next best thing to home. Mason and I don't officially work there, but we all help out when we can.

I followed Mason into the storeroom. It's packed with shipping boxes and instruments that need repairing. Dad was at his desk, writing *Trash* on a piece of paper that he had taped to a sagging black amplifier.

"Wow!" Mason said. "Is that a Skyrocket 3000?"

Dad nodded. "A guy dropped it off for recycling yesterday. Apparently it's broken."

"No *way*," said Mason.

"You want it?" Dad asked.

Mason nodded eagerly, his eyes so wide that you'd think he'd just won a free car. My brother loves rewiring musical gear. Our garage is full of half-fixed amplifiers and soundboards that he's determined to repair.

"Great, we'll bring it home to the workshop after rehearsal," Dad said.

Mason craned his neck to peek out the window.

"I'm not sure we're getting back to rehearsal any time soon," he said. "Jesse's still on the phone."

I groaned.

Dad gave my shoulder a little squeeze. "Tenney, I know you're excited to practice, but Jesse's got a lot of solo shows coming up and she's a little stressed out. So let's just give her another few minutes here."

I knew Jesse was busy, but it was hard to be patient. I'd been looking forward to band rehearsal all week. If I could, I'd play music every waking minute.

"Fine," I said after a moment. "I'll go work on some of my own songs."

"Good idea," Dad said, ruffling my hair.

I ducked out of the storeroom and returned to the small stage at the front of the store. Dad lets customers use the stage to test out microphones, amplifiers, and instruments, and it doubles as the Tri-Stars' rehearsal space. I slung my guitar over my shoulder and adjusted Jesse's microphone to my height, looking out at the empty store. Waylon was curled up by the vintage cash register, watching me. For a moment, I imagined myself on a real stage, in front of thousands of people, about to perform a song I'd written.

"This next one goes out to Waylon," I said into the microphone.

I picked out the chords of the tune I'd been working on. Melody comes easy to me, but it takes me a long time to find the right lyrics to match. I hadn't figured out words to this song yet, so I just hummed the melody while I played. As the song's energy rose and washed over me, I filled the empty room with music.

The song ended and I opened my eyes. Waylon was asleep, which made me laugh. Jesse was still on the phone outside. Everything looked the same, but somehow I felt stronger inside. Playing music always made me feel like that. But performing my *own* songs for people, letting them feel what I felt through the music—*that* was my biggest dream.

Jesse came through the door and tucked her cell phone into her pocket. "Okay," she said. "Go get your dad and brother, and let's get this rehearsal over with."

I snarled and let my fingers ripple down my

guitar's six strings, sending up a wave of notes. *Jesse doesn't know how good she has it singing lead*, I thought. I hopped off the stage and headed toward the storeroom. *Maybe I should ask Dad to let me perform one of my songs with the Tri-Stars*, I thought. But I knew that he'd only agree if he thought the song was *great*. And that meant not playing it for him until I was sure it was ready.

HOT CHICKEN & BRIGHT LIGHTS

Chapter 2

*W*e wrapped up rehearsal and drove home. When we pulled up, my seven-year-old sister, Aubrey, welcomed us by doing cartwheels on the lawn in front of Mom's food truck. I love Mom's truck. It has shiny silver bumpers and it's painted robin's-egg blue. *Georgia's Genuine Tennessee Hot Chicken* is painted in scrolling tomato-red letters along the side.

Mom appeared from the open garage, her carrot-colored hair twisted up under a bandanna, and her freckly arms moving fast as she loaded food bins into the truck's tiny kitchen. She reminded me of a hummingbird: always in motion and stronger than she looks.

"Finally!" Mom said, as we hopped out of Dad's pickup truck. "We were starting to get worried about y'all. How was rehearsal?"

"Okay," I said. "But we only rehearsed three songs."

Mom raised an eyebrow. As the former lead singer of the Tri-Stars, she knew that being in a band is always full of drama. "What happened?" she asked.

"Jesse happened," said Mason.

"We sounded good, though," Dad chimed in.

Aubrey cartwheeled over to us, her sparkly tutu bouncing as she landed with a thud on the grass. "When do I get to play with the Tri-Stars?" she asked.

"Soon, baby," Dad said.

Aubrey pouted. Everyone in my family plays an instrument, but Dad is the one who decides when we're ready to perform with the band. Dad plays anything with strings. Mom sings and plays Autoharp, Mason plays mandolin and drums, and Aubrey's learning accordion. I've played guitar since I was four, and I started banjo last year. Dad always says that as members of the Grant family, we have music in our bones.

HOT CHICKEN & BRIGHT LIGHTS

Mom rubbed Aubrey's shoulder. "Just keep practicing. Nobody ever won a Country Music Award by doing cartwheels onstage." She checked her watch and nodded at my guitar case. "Better get that inside, Tenney. We're wheels up in ten minutes," she said. "We need to be set up by six o'clock."

We were about to take the truck downtown to sell Mom's food at Centennial Park. Aubrey's favorite singer, Belle Starr, would be performing an outdoor concert there. I wasn't a huge fan, but I'd never turn down a chance to hear live music.

I ran into our family room with its red patchwork rug, jumble of antique furniture, and musical instruments everywhere. I set my guitar next to a couple of Dad's and raced upstairs to the bedroom I share with Aubrey. You can definitely tell whose side is whose. Aubrey's half looks like a glitter factory exploded. My side's less shimmery, and decorated with all things music. I've adorned the wall over my bed with old photos of Patsy Cline, Joan Baez, and Johnny Cash, and a framed 78 rpm record of one of my favorite songs, Elvis Presley singing "Hound Dog." My guitar pick collection sits in a glass jar on my nightstand.

As I sat down to change shoes, I saw my most prized possession: my songwriting journal. The cover was decorated with rosebuds and blooms, and I'd covered its pages with lyrics, song ideas, and doodles. With my new melody still stuck in my head, I was tempted to crack open the journal to work out some lyrics. Before I could, though, Mom honked from the driveway. I hopped up with a sigh. Writing my song would have to wait.

Mom turned the food truck onto the parkway out of East Nashville with Mason, Aubrey, and me belted into the food truck's jump seats behind Dad. Before we'd even crossed the bridge over the Cumberland River toward downtown, Aubrey was squirming with boredom.

"Turn on the radio," she pleaded. "Pretty please?"

Mom switched it on. A bubbly electronic beat filled the car.

Aubrey shrieked. "Turn it up, it's Belle Starr!"

We'd all heard the song "Star Like Me" a bazillion times, and I was starting to get a little tired of it. But when Mom turned it up I couldn't keep from bobbing my head to the beat. Aubrey wiggled and sang along with Belle's chorus:

"You can be a star like me! Know who you are and you'll be free. Be proud of yourself and love what you see. That's when you'll see who you can be!"

"Catchy," Dad said to me, over Aubrey's singing.

I nodded. It was easy to see why Belle and the song were a hit. The melody had a bouncy hook— the kind that you can't get out of your head. Clangy guitars twanged under her voice. I thought they sounded fake, as if the sound came from a computer and not real instruments.

"Be proud of yourself and love what you see ... " Aubrey belted. She may have been off-key, but her excitement was infectious.

As I started singing with her, Mom joined in, too. *"Look in the mirror and see what you'll be. If you follow your dream, you'll be a star like me!"*

Mom's voice rang out, clear, creamy, and warm.

She sounded a hundred times better than Belle Starr.

"Can we *please* turn off the cheeseball music?" Mason begged. "It's bad enough that I have to suffer through her concert!"

We giggled and kept on singing. Mason squeezed his hands over his ears until the song ended.

Mom steered the truck onto the roundabout at the edge of Music Row. I craned my neck to peer at the bungalows and office buildings that house some of the most famous record labels and recording studios in Nashville. From Elvis to the Beach Boys to LeAnn Rimes, some of the biggest performers in the world have recorded here. As we drove by, I imagined myself inside one of these historic studios, standing in a recording booth with headphones on, singing a song I'd written. Excitement shivered through me.

We stopped at a red light outside a boxy building marked SILVER SUN, one of the most famous record labels in Music City. In our family, it's beyond legendary.

"Mom, there's Silver Sun Records!" I said.

"That's where you recorded your demo, right?"

Mom pressed her lips into a thin line and nodded. "Yep," she said stiffly. "A long time ago."

"What was it like inside?" I asked. I'd heard the story of Mom's brush with music stardom a dozen times, but it never got old.

"It was . . . memorable," Mom said without looking at the building. When the light turned green, she pressed her foot on the gas and didn't say another word.

Before long, we arrived at Centennial Park. The food trucks were assigned a lot across the lawn from the stage where Belle Starr would be performing. As soon as Mom pulled into our spot, we started setting up. Mason and Dad unpacked drinks and side dishes while Mom heated up the stove and the frying station to cook the chicken to order. Mom makes everything she sells in the food truck herself, but her specialty is traditional Nashville-style hot chicken, spicy and fried and served over a slice of white bread with pickles. Mom uses wild honey, too, so her chicken tastes like sweet, crunchy, peppery bits of heaven.

TENNEY

As I set up the menu board, I glanced over at
Belle Starr's stage. It had been built in front of the
massive white columns of the Parthenon, a replica
of the ancient Greek temple. The lawn was packed
with people who had arrived early to claim space
on the grass to watch the concert.

Everyone is here to see Belle Starr, I thought. *Does
she get nervous when she sings for all those people?*

"Tenney," my mom called, interrupting my
daydream. "Can you help Aubrey with the utensils?
We'll have customers any minute."

Sure enough, just as Aubrey and I set out the
forks and napkins, hungry concertgoers started
gathering around the food trucks.

Dad played a fast tune on his guitar to get
their attention. *"Georgia's Hot Chicken! Georgia's Hot
Chicken! Get some quick before we're all outta pickin's!"*
he howled, strumming wildly.

I joined Dad's song as Aubrey danced around
doing jazz hands. We weren't great, but people
noticed us. Soon we had a line of customers waiting to buy my mom's food.

For the next hour, we worked hard to keep

the customer line moving. As soon as the sky turned dark, the Parthenon's stage lit up in a blaze of lights and electric guitar riffs. I only saw Belle Starr for a split second before the crowd jumped up, blocking my view.

"Hello, Nashville!" Belle Starr called over the sound system. The crowd roared.

"I want to see!" whined Aubrey. Dad put her on his shoulders as the band launched into "Star Like Me."

Mom looked out of the truck, wiping her hands on her apron.

"Sorry about the view, Tenney," she said.

"It's okay," I said. I didn't care that I couldn't see. I just loved being at a concert, the air crackling with excitement. *Live music makes everything brighter,* I thought. When I looked up, it seemed like the stars were dancing.

When Belle Starr finished her song, the audience burst into applause.

"Wow," I said. "The audience really loves her."

Mom nodded but didn't say anything.

"Do you miss performing?" I asked.

She shrugged. "Sometimes."

As Belle Starr dove into her next hit song, I had to yell over the screaming crowd. "I wonder if I'll ever get to play my own music for an audience this big."

"Make the music you love first," she said. "The rest will take care of itself."

I hoped she was right. Because making music was what I wanted to do forever.

THE JAMBOREE

Chapter 3

On Monday morning, Dad dropped me off at school. I started sixth grade at Magnolia Hills Middle School in September. It's much bigger than my elementary school, and even though we were already a month into the semester, I was still getting to know my way around. Luckily, my best friend, Jaya Mitra, is in the same homeroom, so I never felt entirely lost.

I got to class and found Jaya drawing at her desk in the front row. She was wearing bright green pants, a red top, and rainbow barrettes in her black curly hair. When she saw me, her eyes lit up.

"Look!" she said, holding up her binder. On the page, both of our names curved together in elegant, hand-drawn letters. "It's my new font."

"Wow, it's gorgeous!" I said, sitting at my desk behind her.

"Hey, did you get my text yesterday?" she asked. "I sent you a video of a piglet kissing a puppy."

"Yes, it was so cute!" I said, remembering. "Sorry, I meant to write back."

"That's okay," Jaya said. "I thought you could use something funny before your Tri-Stars rehearsal with Jesse. How did it go?"

"Okay," I said with a sigh. Before I could tell her anything more, though, the bell rang, signaling the start of class. Our teacher, Ms. Carter, collected permission slips for our upcoming sixth-grade field trip.

"I know that most of you have been to the Ryman Auditorium before," she told us, "but I promise that this tour will make Nashville's musical history come to life. It's the perfect way to get everyone excited to work on this year's Magnolia Hills Jamboree."

Excitement rippled through the room. The Jamboree is our school's annual autumn carnival. Every year the students plan games, make food, and play live music to celebrate fall. It's a big event for the neighborhood, too. My family had been going for years, and I'd always loved it. It was exciting to think that this year I was going to help put it on!

Ms. Carter smiled. "And while we're on the subject of the Jamboree, I have some exciting news: Normally, the money we raise goes to a local charity," she said, "but this year, we're doing some things differently. We'll be partnering with seniors from the Lillian Street Senior Center to plan the event. Not only that, but the Jamboree itself will take place *at* the center."

My classmates murmured to each other with surprise. Ms. Carter didn't even blink.

"Two members of this class will serve on the Jamboree Steering Committee with representatives from the other homerooms," she said. "We'll come up with ideas for food and stalls. The committee will also be working with seniors at the center to help them get involved. This is a chance for all of you to connect with members of our community. It'll take some after-school time," she added, "but I promise it'll be worth it. Any volunteers?"

Jaya's hand shot up. "Tenney, come on," she whispered.

*It **would** be fun to work on the Jamboree*, I thought, *especially with Jaya*. I raised my hand.

Ms. Carter's eyes scanned the raised hands in the room and landed on the front row. "Tenney and Jaya, thank you for volunteering," said Ms. Carter. "We'll meet here today at lunch."

The fourteen kids on the Jamboree committee were settling into a circle of desks for the meeting when Jaya and I got back from the cafeteria with our lunches. I immediately spotted Holliday Hayes—and got a sour feeling in my stomach. Her purple plaid headband perfectly matched her pencil case and high-top sneakers, as usual. Holliday and I had been in the same class in fifth grade. She'd always been polite to me, but we weren't friends, exactly. She always seemed more interested in being right than in being friends.

As we munched on our sandwiches, Ms. Carter

called the meeting to order. "This year's Jamboree theme is Southern Hospitality," she said. "Who has ideas for food we can serve?"

Suggestions started flying. We all agreed that we should have a stall serving different flavors of sweet tea, and another where you could decorate your own cupcakes.

"My mom makes fresh pralines," said one girl. "She could have a booth."

"Great idea!" Holliday chirped. "And my dad's got the hot chicken covered."

"Tenney's mom makes hot chicken, too," said Jaya. "She has her own food truck."

"It's really good," I said, trying not to sound like I was bragging.

"I'm sure," Holliday said, "but my dad said he'd pay for a cook from Bolton's to come out."

Everyone looked impressed. Bolton's makes Nashville's most famous hot chicken.

"That seems expensive," Ms. Carter said.

"It's all right," replied Holliday. "My dad really wants to do it."

"Well, if your father insists," Ms. Carter said.

A smug grin wreathed Holliday's face. I couldn't help feeling a little disappointed. But I told myself that Mom would probably rather *attend* the Jamboree than *work* there.

"Now, moving on to entertainment," said Ms. Carter. "We want students and seniors performing all day, so if any of you dance or act or play music, think about signing up."

Excitement fizzed inside me. This could be my chance to perform my own songs!

Holliday's voice broke into my thoughts. "My dad's a vice president at Silver Sun Records," she said. "That's Belle Starr's label. I could ask if she's free."

Now everyone *really* looked excited.

"You can get Belle Starr to come?" squeaked a blond boy.

Ms. Carter stepped in. "Actually, Holliday, the Jamboree is about showcasing musicians from the East Nashville community."

Holliday shrugged.

"A sign-up sheet for performers will go on my door after lunch," Ms. Carter continued, looking around the room. "Don't wait to put down your name, though. Slots fill up fast, and we always have a big crowd."

"You *have* to sign up!" Jaya whispered to me.

I managed a smile. But the thought of performing for almost everyone in school was making my stomach do somersaults.

"Now," Ms. Carter added, "this committee needs a chairperson. Who'd like to volunteer to lead us?"

Jaya and Holliday both shot their hands into the air. Ms. Carter asked them both to tell the group why they wanted to be chairperson and then we'd vote. Jaya went first.

"Improving our community is really important to me, and I think working with the senior center is a great way for us to get more involved with our neighbors," Jaya said. "I love working on a team and coming up with ideas together. I think that's the best way to face a challenge."

Ms. Carter smiled. "Very nice, Jaya. Now, Holliday. Tell us why you think you'd make a good chairperson."

Holliday sat up very tall. "I want to be chair-person because I have really good ideas," she said. "I'm good at making decisions and keeping track of what everyone should be doing. Also I promise, if I'm elected, this Jamboree will have more cup-cakes than any other Jamboree in the history of the school."

"Wow," said Ms. Carter. "That's a tall order! Thank you both."

We put our heads on our desks and raised our hands to vote. I voted for Jaya, of course.

"The votes are in!" Ms. Carter announced. "The sixth-grade chairperson is . . . Holliday Hayes!"

Holliday stood up and beamed. "Thank you all so much for making the right choice."

I looked over at Jaya. She put on a brave smile as she congratulated Holliday, but her eyes looked sad. As we dumped our lunch trash, I could tell she was upset.

"I should have said something about cupcakes, too," she said.

I tried to think of something that would cheer her up. "Well, we'll still have fun working on the

Jamboree," I said. "Maybe you could volunteer to design the posters."

Jaya perked up. "Good idea," she said. "Are you going to sign up to perform?"

"Maybe," I said. "I've only played with the Tri-Stars, though. I've never performed alone onstage. What if I mess up?"

"You won't!" said Jaya, giving me a squeeze. "You're a great singer. Plus, you've got six weeks until the Jamboree."

"That would give me time to practice," I admitted.

"Yes!" she said. "I bet you could even write a new song, if you wanted."

Maybe Jaya was right. The new song I'd been working on had a *really* great melody. If I could nail the lyrics, I knew it would be amazing.

I could play a real solo show as a singer-songwriter! My heart did an excited drumroll. I smiled until a worrying thought hit me: *What if I play and no one thinks my songs are any good?*

I decided I'd take some time to think about it.

LILLIAN STREET SENIOR CENTER

Chapter 4

*O*n Thursday, the Jamboree committee visited the Lillian Street Senior Center for the first time. As the center director showed us around, he pointed through a window at a spacious brick patio and sprawling green lawn lined with trees. "We're planning to build a stage out there," he told us, "and arrange the food and craft stalls around it."

"We should string lights across, too," said Holliday Hayes.

"Good idea!" said Ms. Carter. "We'll figure out more of the details later. But now it's time to get the seniors involved," she said.

The center director smiled and nodded. "Having the Jamboree here will help our seniors stay actively involved in the community," he said.

"They can hardly contain their excitement about this event."

"Each of you needs to find a senior to partner with," said Ms. Carter. "Spend some time getting to know each other, and then ask your partner how they'd like to be involved with the Jamboree. Ideally, you will be partners at the event, too."

We headed into the main activity room. Older people were sitting at tables and on couches, reading, chatting, and playing board games. For a moment, we all looked at one another awkwardly.

I suddenly felt a little shy. What could I possibly have in common with someone my grandmother's age?

"Come on, y'all, hop to it!" Ms. Carter said.

Jaya immediately stepped forward and approached a man wearing rainbow suspenders. Following her lead, the rest of us spread across the room. Holliday marched up to a woman in a pink jumpsuit and matching lipstick. I started toward an older man with kind eyes and a bowtie, but one of my classmates reached him first. In a blink, it seemed as if all the seniors had partners.

Finally, I spotted a woman with messy gray hair huddled in a deep chair in the corner of the room, frowning as she peered out the window. She didn't look friendly, but she was my only choice.

"Excuse me, ma'am?" I said as I approached.

The woman glanced at me with watery blue eyes. I greeted her, but I'd barely even gotten out the word "Jamboree" before she turned toward the window again.

"I think it will be a lot of fun," I said. "So would you be my partner?"

"I suppose," she replied, so sourly that you'd think I was asking her to eat boiled okra.

"Great!" I said, pasting on a smile. "I'm Tenney. What's your name?"

She hesitated, as if she was trying to decide whether she should trust me.

"Portia," she said finally.

"Okay," I said. "Um, what do you like to do for fun?"

"Backgammon and general thinking," she retorted.

General thinking and backgammon didn't

seem like good activities for Jamboree stalls. I couldn't think of what to say next, though, so we just sat there.

I glanced around. Everyone else was chatting easily with their senior partners. I decided I wasn't going to give up on mine just yet.

"We're doing a bake sale. Do you bake?" I asked.

Portia shook her head. "I like eating, though," she said, with a small smile.

Encouraged, I kept asking questions. Portia mostly gave one-word answers and seemed far away, as if she was thinking about something more important.

When it was time to go, I said good-bye to Portia and followed the other members of the Jamboree committee toward the entrance of the senior center. When I glanced back, I was surprised to see Portia looking directly at me with a curious expression. I waved to her, and she gave a slow wave back.

"The Jamboree is going to be super fun!" Jaya said as we walked home. She told me about her senior partner, the rainbow-suspenders man. His name was Frank and he used to work at a newspaper. Together they'd come up with the idea of having a block-printing booth at the Jamboree.

"Frank knows someone who'll lend us a portable printing press!" she said with a skip. "I'm going to design a limited-edition Jamboree poster. Then at the event, we'll show people how to print them!"

"Sounds cool," I said. "And Frank sounds really great." Jaya's enthusiasm made me wish Portia and I had connected like she had with Frank.

"How did it go with your partner, Tenney?" she asked, almost as if she was reading my mind.

"Okay," I said, "but I'm not really sure that Portia likes talking to me."

"She just needs to get to know you," Jaya said, hooking her arm with mine. "Maybe next time, you should try to figure out what you two have in common—like Frank and I did."

"Good idea," I said, relieved to have a plan.

That night, after dinner, dishes, and home-work, I finally had time to work on my music. I grabbed my guitar and my songwriting journal and headed to the backyard. The air was crisp as Waylon followed me down the porch steps to my favorite spot to write: a soft patch of grass next to his doghouse under the wide oak tree. I sat down and took a big breath. All during dinner, my new melody had been bouncing around my head. Now I wanted to focus. I flipped through my journal to the page where I'd been brainstorming lyrics for the song.

Aubrey calls my journal a "diary," which bugs me. She says it like I just write about boys and other drama and draw hearts and butterflies everywhere. There are a few doodles, but mostly I write down song ideas. Anyone else looking at it would prob-ably just see a scribbled mess of words and chord progressions, but to me the pages are a collection of puzzle pieces, each one waiting for the moment when I can fit it into a song.

I stared down at my lyrics brainstorm. So far, I had clusters of words and the start of two lines:

This song's for you, my love.
You watch over me from above.

I wrinkled my nose. "From above" sounded weird, like "my love" was on the roof or something—or was dead. That's *definitely* not what I wanted to say. *I need a word that rhymes with love,* I thought.

Who looks like a sweet white dove?

No way, I thought, frowning.

Whose arms fit me like a glove?

Who gives me a big shove?

Ugh, NO!

And who was "my love" anyway?

I squeezed my eyes shut with frustration. No matter how much I loved my melody, I couldn't come up with lyrics until I'd figured out what it was *about.* I opened my eyes. Moths danced around the porch light. Inside the lit kitchen, I could see my parents talking.

Maybe I should ask Mom or Dad for some ideas, I thought. They're practically experts when it comes to songwriting. Unfortunately, they have the same rule about songwriting that they do with homework: I can't ask them for help until I've finished on my own. If I told Dad I was having problems with a song now, he'd just give me his crooked smile and quote his favorite line of *Ulysses,* by Alfred, Lord Tennyson, the poet I was named after.

"'To strive, to seek, to find, and not to yield,'" he'd say. "Songwriting's hard. But this is a song by Tennyson Evangeline Grant. That means something. Your music, your voice. That means *your* words."

If I asked Mom, I knew she would remind me that I'm still trying to find my voice. "The best songs come from people who dig deep to figure out how they feel and then write about it," she always says. "Nobody can do that for you but you."

The sound of the creaking screen door interrupted my thoughts. I glanced up and saw that Mom was on the porch.

"Time for bed, Dreamy," she said.

Mom always calls me Dreamy when I'm songwriting because I block out everything around me and get lost in the musical world inside my head.

I glanced down at my journal. I was so tired that the words on the page were blurring together. I sighed and hopped up.

"There's always tomorrow," Mom said as I came up the porch steps. "No song was built in a day."

CENTER STAGE

Chapter 5

*T*hat Saturday, Dad, Mason, and I loaded our instruments into Dad's pickup and headed over to East Park, where the Neighborhood Association mixer was happening. The Tri-Stars were performing at two o'clock—a whole hour from now—but I could hardly wait to get onstage.

East Park's small, just a square of grass and a few playing fields. A temporary stage had been set up on the baseball diamond, where another local band was playing a lively bluegrass tune for a small crowd. A few dozen people were milling around two food stalls. Mom could have sold hot chicken, I thought, but she'd taken the truck and Aubrey to work a private party. We spotted some of our neighbors, and Dad stopped to say hello to Ms. Pavone, the woman with enormous purple glasses who lives next door.

Finally, we circled up behind the stage and tuned our instruments. Dad went over the set list, naming each song in the order we were going to play them. By the time he was done, I could tell Mason was getting nervous—Jesse still hadn't arrived.

"We go on in less than a half hour," Mason said, checking his watch. "Where is she?"

Dad pressed his lips together. "I'll call her," he said. He whipped out his phone and dialed, shaking his head when she didn't answer. He tried again a few minutes later—and then again . . .

By the time she picked up, we were supposed to go on in fifteen minutes. I couldn't hear what Dad was telling her, but he did not look happy. When he hung up and walked back to us, he looked dazed.

"Is she on her way?" I asked.

"No," Dad said. "She quit."

Mason and I gasped.

"Now?" I squeaked. "No way! She can't!"

"It's okay," Dad said, although he didn't *look* okay. "We can reorganize the set list. I'll sing lead."

"What about 'Carolina Highway' and 'Wildwood Flower'?" Mason said, with worry creasing
his forehead. "Your voice is too low—and we've
never practiced those songs in another key."

"I can sing them!" I blurted out, without even
thinking.

Dad gave me a worried squint.

"I can," I insisted. "I have the same range
as Jesse, and I've sung both songs in rehearsal
a million times."

"Tenney's right—she can do it," Mason said.

A nervous chill tap-danced down my back.
This was all happening so fast. "What about my
guitar part?" I asked. "I can't sing and play backup
too—not without rehearsing."

"I'll play guitar and we'll do without bass for
'Carolina Highway,'" Dad decided. "All you need to
do is sing."

I took a deep breath and tried to ignore my
galloping heart. "Okay," I said.

Dad looked relieved, and Mason squeezed my
shoulder.

I can't believe it, I thought. *I'm actually going to*

sing lead! Excitement tingled through me. But when I looked up at the crowd dancing in front of the stage, my confidence suddenly evaporated. I'd sung solos, but I'd never sung a whole song alone in front of an audience. And now I was going to sing *two*. I took a deep breath.

I know these songs. It'll be fine.

The next few minutes were a blur. We ran through both song intros so I'd remember when to start singing, and then waited for the act ahead of us to finish. Finally, we went onstage.

I tried not to look at the audience as I helped set up our gear with Mason and Dad. I didn't want to be reminded of how many people were going to be looking at me.

Once we were ready, Dad stepped up to the lead microphone. "Ladies and gentlemen, we are the Tennessee Tri-Stars, named for our beautiful state flag," he said with a smile. "We're one star short today, but I've got faith that we're still going to shine."

He gave me a wink and counted off. We jumped into our set. Our first two songs were fast and fun, designed to get people dancing. Dad calls this trick "lighting up the audience." By the time Dad started his guitar solo on "The Devil Went Down to Georgia," people were clapping to the beat. Dad's fingers flew. He was playing so fast I thought his strings might start smoking! As he finished with a flourish, people shouted, "Bravo!"

How am I supposed to follow that?! I thought.

We were playing "Carolina Highway" next. Dad had originally written it for Mom to sing, years ago. It's a great song, but it needed a voice as good as hers. I tried to swallow my anxiety.

Just stay on key, I told myself.

"I'm so proud to introduce the youngest Tri-Star," Dad said. "My daughter, Tenney."

Dad moved over, and I stepped up to the lead microphone. It was too high, but before I could ask Dad to adjust it, he started playing. Mason joined in, his mandolin balancing Dad's rhythm guitar.

I can do this, I told myself.

My cue was approaching. I tried to pull the microphone toward my mouth—but it didn't budge.

It's locked! I realized, panicking. I tried to loosen

the knob, but it was no use. How was anyone going to hear me?!

I yanked the mic again with both hands, but it stayed put. Finally, just in time for my cue, I pulled the mic out of its clip and stepped around the stand.

"*This Carolina highway's full of dead ends and byways,*" I sang. "*This Carolina highway's awfully dark. It twists into forever. I might be heading nowhere—I just hope it leads me back into your heart.*"

Okay, got through that one. Eight bars later, I sang the second verse even better than the first, my voice becoming clearer as I gained confidence. Now came the chorus. Mason and Dad got ready to harmonize with me.

"*Where are you?*" I sang, relaxing into my usual singing part. Then I had a horrified thought: *No one's singing the melody.*

I was so startled I went quiet, missing the next lyric.

"*I need you,*" Mason and Dad sang together, covering for me.

Embarrassment turned my cheeks hot, and I

turned around to look at Dad. His eyes locked on mine. *I believe in you*, his look said.

I gave a nod and breathed deeply. *Stay in the moment*, I told myself. It didn't seem like the crowd had noticed my screwup. People were listening politely. Ms. Pavone gave me an encouraging thumbs-up. As the next verse started, I put my heart into it.

"Carolina highway, are you going my way?" I sang. I closed my eyes, my voice sailing across the melody. *"Carolina highway, help me just fly away."*

My nerves melted away. I opened my eyes. Why had I been so afraid? The audience was swaying to the rhythm. I felt like I was being held up by love.

The chorus started again. *"Where are you?"* I sang, looking up at the sky. I felt strong and free, more like myself than I ever had before. I never wanted the song to end.

But when it did, the crowd burst into applause.

"Thank you," I whispered into the mic.

Before I could take in the moment, Dad started playing "Wildwood Flower." It's a simple folk song, and I've practiced it a lot, so it was easier than "Carolina Highway." Singing it felt like hanging out with a good friend.

Somewhere in the middle of the song, I glanced over at Dad. He was watching me, looking proud and a bit stunned, as if he hadn't really seen me before this moment.

For the rest of the show, I felt like I was floating. I'd done it! I'd sung lead, and I sounded *good*! I just wished Mom had been there to see it. I couldn't wait to tell her everything.

When we got home, I rushed inside. Mom was in the living room with Waylon. She listened patiently as we told her how I'd ended up singing lead.

"Congratulations, honey," Mom said. "Did you have fun?"

"I had *so* much fun!" I said.

"Tenney was fantastic," Dad said.

"*Better* than fantastic," Mason said, throwing

himself onto the couch next to Waylon.

"Could I sing lead again sometime?" I asked.

Mom laughed. "Well, it sounds like you might get more chances now," she said, raising an eyebrow at Dad.

"Just don't start singing any old where," Dad said.

"I won't," I said, but I barely heard him. My mind was still buzzing with excitement.

I couldn't wait to perform again.

ELLIE CALE

Chapter 6

*T*he next morning, I was back at Dad's
store, helping to restock guitar strings. As
I slipped the packets onto their hooks, moments
from the Tri-Stars show kept replaying in my
head. Not only had I gotten through both songs
without making any huge mistakes, I'd had *fun*
singing lead. The only thing that would have
made the experience even better was if I'd sung
a song I'd written.

*Singing my own songs, I could really show people
who I am*, I thought. *And with the right lyrics, I could
maybe make them feel what I feel.* I pictured the crowd
singing along with my song, everybody thinking
about how the lyrics related to their own lives. With
that image in my mind, I was more motivated than
ever to finish my new song.

I looked up at my dad, who was punching numbers into a calculator behind the cash register. "Dad, can I take a break?" I asked. "I want to work on a new song."

"Sure, honey," he said. "I think the listening room is available if you want to practice on your favorite guitar."

I flashed him a grin. The guitar I own, the one I use to write songs and perform with the Tri-Stars, is what musicians call a "beater." It's plain and old, with scratches above the sound hole and on the pick guard. It's not a beauty, but it sounds good, and in music, that's what counts—right?

But ever since Dad got a new shipment of guitars in the store, I had fallen in love with one in particular—a mini Taylor with white rosebuds and vines swirling around its aquamarine body, and a single songbird perched on its bridge.

I skipped over to the guitar display room and slipped it off the wall before heading to my favorite part of the shop: a small wood-lined "listening room" in the back where you can play any guitar you want in private. It's where my dad taught me how to play guitar. Most of what I know about music, I learned in this little room.

I closed the door and started working on my song. First, I played slowly through the melody. There are lots of ways to put together a song, but this one was pretty straightforward. It had two verses, then a chorus and a bridge—a section in the middle of the song with a different melody and lyrics to keep the listener's attention—and the final chorus.

"La-la-la-la," I sang, since I still didn't have any lyrics. "La-la-laaa . . ."

Hearing the melody made me fall in love with the song all over again. It was simple but heartfelt, and it sounded great on this guitar, which had a richer sound than my old beater. I picked up the tempo, feeling the joy and heartache the melody stirred up inside me.

A knock on the listening room's window startled me. I jumped and dropped my pick. A young woman with spiky dark hair stood on the other side of the window. She was wearing a retro-looking pink shawl over a tank top and jeans. A line of tiny hoop earrings sparkled on the curve of one ear.

I opened the door to the listening room. "Sorry," I said. "Do you want to use the room?"

"Actually, I wanted to talk to you," she replied. "You're really good. What song were you playing?"

"Oh, um . . . it doesn't have a name yet," I said, startled.

The woman's eyebrows shot straight up. "Did you write it?" she asked.

I nodded.

"Really," she said. She leaned in, squinting at me like I was a bug or something. "I think I saw you perform yesterday at East Park."

"Yes!" I said proudly. "It's our family band. We're called the Tri-Stars."

Before she could reply, Mason came up behind her. "Can I help you?" he asked. "Or was my little sister playing too loud again?" He gave me a wink.

"I'd like to hear more, actually," said the woman, turning back to me. "I was just telling your sister here how much I liked her song."

Mason nodded. "Tenney's our little star," he said, making me blush.

"Well, it's nice to meet you, Tenney," she said, shaking my hand. "My name is Ellie." She reached into her purse and handed me a card.

"Ellie Cale," I read aloud. "A&R Coordinator, Mockingbird Records." My heart skipped a beat.

"Mockingbird *Records*?" Mason repeated.

"Tenney, I think you're a great performer," she told me. "You have a unique voice, solid guitar chops, and great stage presence. I knew you had something special when I saw you play yesterday at East Park, but now that I know you wrote that song—" She paused and nodded thoughtfully.

I held my breath, waiting for her to finish her thought.

At last she said, "Are you interested in pursuing a career in music? From what I've seen so far, I think you have a lot of potential."

My jaw felt like it dropped to the ground, I was so surprised.

"You know she's twelve, right?" Mason blurted.

"Mason," I snarled, glaring at him.

ELLIE CALE

Ellie chuckled. "Tenney, have you written any other songs?"

"I have a few, but—"

Mason interrupted me. "She writes all the time. She's really talented."

"Great! We're always looking for new artists who write their own songs," Ellie continued. "Twice a year Mockingbird hosts a new talent showcase at the Bluebird Cafe. It's a chance for us and some other labels and management to hear undiscovered talent. Our next showcase is in a month. Would you like to come and play an original song for us?"

"Yes," I blurted, before I could even process Ellie's question. My brain started racing. The Bluebird Cafe? It's one of the most famous music clubs in Nashville. Everyone from Garth Brooks to Faith Hill has played there. Taylor Swift was *discovered* during one of their songwriter nights. Just thinking about performing there gave me chills. I'd have to rework one of my old songs or finish my new one, but I could do it. I *had* to do it!

"Great," said Ellie. "Double-check to make sure your parents are cool with it, and then give me a call to confirm you'll be there. Okay?"

I nodded so hard my teeth chattered.

After Ellie left, Mason and I ran to the front of the store to tell Dad about Ellie's offer.

"Wow," he said, "that is something."

"It's more than something—it's amazing!" Mason said. He picked me up and spun me around.

Dad laughed, but it was hard to tell what he was thinking. "We'll talk about it with your mom tonight," he said.

As soon as we got home, Mason told Mom I'd been "scouted."

Dad showed Mom Ellie's card. "Mockingbird Records is a solid label," he said.

"That is true," Mom said, handing me silverware to set the table for dinner. She didn't seem as excited as I expected. She barely said anything when Mason looked up Mockingbird Records on the Internet and rattled off the names of some of the great artists they had signed.

"What if after Tenney sings at the showcase, Mockingbird decides to *sign* her?!" he said.

My heart did a pirouette in my chest.

My parents looked up at each other but didn't say a word. Mom just handed the dinner rolls to Aubrey and said, "Will you put these on the table, sweetie?"

Why aren't they more excited? I wondered. I thought of Mom's story about recording a demo with Silver Sun Records.

"What if they let me make a demo—and then they decide to turn it into a record? And what if when it comes out, it's a hit?" I asked, my mouth moving faster than my brain. I did an excited spin and bumped into Aubrey and her rolls.

"Watch it," she said with a frown, and set down the breadbasket.

"Sor-ry!" I sang, dancing away.

"Okay, Tenney," Mom said, sounding amused. "Let's not get too far out in front of this. It's an invitation to a showcase."

"But it could be the first step to becoming a professional musician!" I cried.

My parents exchanged another tiny, cautious look.

"What's wrong?" I said, sensing that something was up.

"Honey, we just think you might be a little young for something like this," Dad said.

"Yeah," Aubrey chimed in. I shot her a glare.

"Why am I too young? You were okay with me singing lead with the Tri-Stars! It's just another performance," I said.

"It's more than that," Mom replied, gently. "You said it yourself—it could lead to bigger professional music opportunities for you. And that's something that we need to consider carefully, as your parents."

I felt like I was a balloon that someone had just popped.

"Are you saying I can't play at the showcase?" I said.

"We're saying we need to discuss it in private," Dad responded.

"I don't understand," I said to Mom. "You played professionally. You even recorded a demo!"

"I was a lot older than you at the time, sweet-heart," Mom said gently.

"But I really want to perform at the showcase," I insisted.

"I know," Mom said. She squeezed my shoulder. "Give your father and me a few days to think about this."

FIND YOUR VOICE

Chapter 7

"*You can be a star like me!*" Aubrey wailed, eyes closed. "*Know who you are and you'll be free!*" She had been listening to "Star Like Me" on repeat on Mom's phone ever since we'd all piled into the food truck to drive to school. She was wearing earbuds, so I couldn't hear the actual music, just her voice. That almost made it worse.

I clapped my hands over my ears and stared at my songwriting journal. I'd been trying to brainstorm lyrics for my new song. It had been an entire day since Ellie Cale had invited me to perform at the showcase, and my parents had made it clear that they needed more time to make their decision. I was desperate for an answer—but for now all I could do was focus on my music and try not to think about it.

FIND YOUR VOICE

So far, it hadn't been easy. I still had only two lines:

This song's for you, my love.
You watch over me from above.

I squinted at the words and realized that I disliked them even more than I had a few nights ago. They were sugar sweet and boring, the kind of lines I wrote when I didn't know *what* to write. I crossed out the lyrics with a thick black line.

Maybe this shouldn't be a love song, I told myself. *Except the melody **sounds** like a love song.* I sighed. All my favorite songs were about heartbreak. But what did I know about *that*? I was only in sixth grade!

"*Be proud of yourself and love what you see!*" Aubrey shrieked.

"Mom, make her stop!" Mason groaned.

We stopped at a light. Mom turned to look at Aubrey. "Honey, you've maxed out your Belle Starr time," she said, and put out her hand.

Pouting, Aubrey handed over the phone. Without music, she became restless. She leaned

over, trying to read my journal. I pulled it to
my chest.

"Are you even writing anything?" Aubrey
asked.

"Yes," I said with a scowl. But as I stared at my
scratched-out lyrics, my stomach scrunched up in
frustration.

I need some time alone to write, I thought. *Maybe
after school.*

"Don't forget, Tenney, you have a Jamboree
meeting at the senior center this afternoon," Mom
said, like she was reading my mind.

Oh yeah. I'd forgotten all about that. For now,
my song would have to wait.

When I got to school, I found Jaya at her locker.
Her eyes lit up as I told her about meeting Ellie Cale
and the invitation to perform at the Mockingbird
Records showcase at the Bluebird.

"It's not anything real yet," I said, but Jaya was
already hugging me.

"What do you mean?! It's *incredible!*" she shrieked.

I nodded shyly, but my heart soared with pride. "Don't get too excited yet," I said. "My parents have to agree to let me perform first."

"They will," Jaya said. "They *know* how talented you are. Why would they want to hold you back?"

Jaya's enthusiasm flooded me with hope. My parents had brought music into my life—there's no way they would take it away now.

After school, we met Ms. Carter and the rest of the Jamboree committee outside the school's front doors and walked over to the senior center together.

As soon as we got there, I marched up to Portia, who was sitting in the same armchair where she'd been last time, looking out the window.

"Hi, Portia," I said, trying to warm her up with a smile. "Have you thought about what we could do for the Jamboree?"

"Not really," she said, resting her chin in a

bony hand. Her fingertips were rough and hard. Suddenly, I realized that we had more in common than I thought.

"Do you play guitar?" I asked.

Portia blinked as if she was just waking up. "I do. Why?" she asked.

"You've got calluses on your left hand just like mine," I said, showing her my fingertips. "And I got them from playing my guitar all the time."

She gave a little snort and studied me. "How long have you played?" she asked.

"Since I was four," I replied.

"Are you any good?" she asked, crossing her arms.

I chuckled nervously. "Um, I think so."

"Okay, then," Portia said. She stood up unsteadily and grabbed a carved walking stick from behind the chair. "Follow me," she said, leaning on her stick, and walked haltingly toward a doorway.

I followed her down a hall and into a small book-lined study. Portia eased herself into a leather chair and nodded toward the corner of the room, where a guitar case stood propped against the wall.

"Play something for me," she said.

I never turn down the opportunity to pick up a guitar, but suddenly I felt a little bashful. I set the case on a side table and opened it. Inside was a polished mahogany guitar. Thin lines of inlaid gold sparkled around the sound hole and across the frets.

"Wow," I said. "Is this your guitar?"

Portia nodded.

"It's beautiful," I said.

"That better not stop you from playing it," Portia said.

My stomach fluttered, but I sat down opposite her, pulling the guitar onto my lap. I tuned it and strummed some riffs. The strings sounded light and silvery. The guitar's neck was a little wider than I was used to, but I could still change chords pretty easily.

I slipped into my new melody, pouring my heart into every chord. Portia listened, tapping a finger in time as I played.

When I finished, I looked up at her. Her eyes

shone with a warmth that I hadn't seen before. "That's good," she said. "You wrote that?"

I nodded, surprised. "How did you know?"

"You're playing like the tune's part of you," Portia said. She smiled as my cheeks reddened. "Tell me what the song's about."

"I don't really know yet," I admitted. "I started writing lyrics, but I don't like them."

"Hmm," said Portia. "In my experience, a good song is always about something meaningful to you. Deep down, you already know what it is. You just need to find it."

"Have you written songs before?" I asked, handing her the guitar.

"Some," she said. "But that was a while ago. Tell me more about you."

As she asked questions, answers poured out of me. I told her about the Tri-Stars and singing lead at last weekend's show, and about Ellie Cale and her invitation to the showcase.

"But my parents might not let me perform. They think I'm too young," I said.

"There's no such thing as too young in music,"

Portia said bluntly. "It's not about age; it's about being ready."

"How do you know when you're ready?" I asked.

"When you find your voice," said Portia. She leaned in, her eyes sparkling. "Don't worry about playing one showcase," she said. "You need to figure out what you want to *say* with your music. When you know that, you'll find your voice as an artist. And *that* is something special. That's something no one can ever take away from you."

Portia's advice echoed in my head as I walked back to school with the Jamboree committee. I wanted to find my voice more than anything. But *how*?

"Are you okay?" Jaya asked, nudging me out of my daydream.

"I'm stuck on the words to my new song," I admitted. "How can I write a song I *love* if I don't know what I want to say?"

"Well, if you're stuck, maybe you should take a break from that one," Jaya said, tilting her head. "Whenever I'm having trouble with a design, it always helps me to work on something else."

As soon as she said it, I realized she was right. After all, I wasn't going to find my voice with just one song.

SUNDAY SUPPER

Chapter 8

Every afternoon for the rest of that week, I pored over my songwriting journal after I'd finished my homework. I didn't like most of my old songs anymore, but there was one that I thought might have potential, called "Home Again." I'd written it last year after we got back from a road trip to Knoxville. It wasn't perfect, but it could work if my parents let me play the Mockingbird showcase.

Be patient, I told myself. *And focus on your music.*

By the end of the weekend, though, I was starting to get antsy—my parents *still* hadn't brought up the showcase. I decided that if they didn't give me their decision by dinner, I was going to bring it up.

Tonight was Sunday Supper, a monthly Grant family tradition. We all chipped in to help: I made the salad, Mason prepared the grits, Dad barbecued ribs, Mom baked cornbread and banana pudding pie, and Aubrey set the table on the backyard patio. I usually love Sunday Supper, but that night I felt prickly and worried thinking about the showcase. I needed to know my parents' decision.

Near the end of dinner, everyone was in a good mood and I finally felt brave enough to bring up performing at the showcase. "We should probably call Ellie Cale soon," I said casually. "You know, to let her know whether or not I'm performing."

My parents exchanged a glance. Finally, Dad spoke. "Mom and I talked about this for a long while," he said, "and we don't think it's a good idea for you to play in the showcase."

I sucked in a short breath. "But it's just one performance," I said.

"It's not about the performance," Mom replied. "It's about what it could lead to."

I stared at my plate. If I looked at my mom, I might start crying.

"What about the Jamboree?" Dad asked. "Playing music at your school is a great place to start. We're happy to give you permission to perform there."

"The showcase is hosted by a *music label*, Dad. It could be my big break," I said. I could feel my chin quivering. It took all the strength I had not to fall apart.

"I'm sorry, honey," Mom said, "but we think you're too young to start pursuing a professional music career."

"There's no such thing as too young in music," I fired back, quoting Portia. "It's not about age; it's about being ready."

My parents looked surprised. *Good*, I thought. *Maybe they finally understand . . .* But when they didn't respond, I knew that the conversation was over.

As I took my plate inside, I heard Mason say, "I don't know why you guys won't just let her perform. Chances are, it won't lead to anything. And even if it does, you could say no then. But she's *good* and she deserves—"

"Mason, enough," Dad said.

I dumped my plate and went into the family room. The chairs were set up in a circle for our Sunday music jam, where we all play songs together.

The last thing I wanted to do was pretend everything was okay and play music as a big happy
family. But I knew my parents were not going to let
me off the hook.

Once the dishes were cleared, we settled in the
family room with our instruments.

"Tenney, you want to choose a song first?"
Dad asked, tuning his guitar.

I shook my head. I knew Dad was giving me
first choice to make me feel better, but I wasn't in
the mood.

"Okay, then. Georgia? Do you have one?" Dad
asked Mom.

"I think so," Mom said brightly, slipping her
Autoharp onto her lap. Her fingers skimmed across
the body, picking out the opening chords of "April
Springs."

"Last April the rains came down," she sang, *"and
washed away your love."* Her voice was strong and
woodsy against the shimmering Autoharp, and on
the next line, she looked right at me. *"Last April the
rains came down, and washed away my pride."*

I was still upset, but somehow hearing Mom's

steady voice soothed my hurt feelings. Dad joined in, and their harmony wrapped around me like a warm hug. Still, I wasn't ready to sing.

Mom started the next verse. Dad says my voice is like hers, but as I listened, I couldn't see how that was possible. Mom's voice seemed bigger than her body, as if the song coming out of her was powered by a swirl of emotions. Every note gave me chills.

She could have been a professional, I thought. *What **really** happened at Silver Sun Records? What wasn't she telling me?*

By the time the chorus started and Mason and Aubrey joined in, my frustration had softened and I finally felt ready to play along. As I sang, I felt the aching and loss in the song's lyrics, and I poured my own sadness into my voice. It made me feel better. I was still sad, but I felt connected to my parents, and to Mason and Aubrey—as if the music made us all part of something bigger.

We played song after song, until Aubrey started yawning. Dad took her upstairs to get ready for bed, and Mason went to work on his broken amp in the garage. That left me to help Mom do dishes.

I rinsed the plates, and Mom put them in the dishwasher. We stayed quiet for a long time, but every so often Mom would give me a sideways glance.

"I'm sorry that you feel hurt by our decision," she said finally, drying her hands on a dish towel.

"I'm just confused," I said. "I mean, you recorded a demo yourself. And you wanted a music career."

"I did," she said. "But then I learned that a career in music is not all it's cracked up to be."

"What do you mean?" I asked, frowning.

"Honey, I grew up singing and playing and loving music, just like you," Mom said. "And when I was nineteen, I met a producer who told me I could be a star."

"Then what?" I asked.

Mom leaned against the counter. "Well, sometimes what you start out wanting and what you end up getting turn out to be different things," she said sadly. "I loved music, but I didn't love what the music business did to me."

"What did it do to you?" I asked.

Mom hesitated. "Being a professional musician

can be a lot of pressure, Tenney," she said finally. "It isn't always fun."

I frowned. What could be more fun than doing the thing you love most *all* the time?

Before I could ask, Mom put her hands on my shoulders. "You are incredibly talented, sweetheart," she said. "But being successful in music isn't just about talent—it's about hard work. You're so young. I just want you to be a kid while you still can be. There's no reason to rush into a music career, I promise."

Mom wrapped me up in a hug. I knew she wanted me to feel better, but a question echoed in my mind: *What if I never get a chance like this again?*

IN THE
SPOTLIGHT

Chapter 9

*T*he next day was the sixth grade's field trip
to the Ryman Auditorium. Before the first
bell rang, kids were swarming the bus by the front
steps. Jaya and I boarded and sat near the back.

I leaned against the seat and looked out the
window. I'd had a hard time falling asleep last night
after my talk with Mom. I still couldn't understand
why Mom had been so unhappy as a professional
musician. She had never really answered any of my
questions.

Jaya's voice broke into my thoughts. "What do
you think of this for a Jamboree poster?"

She held up her sketchbook, showing me a colorful drawing of people dancing in front of a big-top
tent. In cowboy-style type, she'd written *Food! Folks!
Fun! Magnolia Hills Jamboree!* across the bottom.

"It's awesome!" I said, pasting on a smile even though I was still feeling down.

Jaya grinned. "Oh, I almost forgot!" she said, flipping to a new page. "I made something for you."

She held it up. *Tenney Grant* was written across the page using a lettering like nothing I'd seen before. The words were written on a five-line staff, like sheet music. The T in Tenney was shaped like a treble clef, and the G was shaped like a bass clef. The rest of the letters looked like musical notes.

"It's your own font!" said Jaya. "You can use it for posters and your website when you start per-forming. What do you think?"

My heart sank. "It's really cool," I said, trying to sound excited, but before I knew it my eyes had filled with tears.

"What's wrong?" Jaya asked.

I took a deep breath and told her all about my parents' decision not to let me play the showcase.

"Oh, Tenney," Jaya said, leaning into me. "I'm so sorry."

Before she could say anything else, the bus came to a stop in front of the Ryman and my classmates started filing into the aisle.

"Try to have fun today, okay?" Jaya said. "You love the Ryman!"

I nodded and gave her a grateful squeeze.

We piled off the bus in the shadow of the majestic red brick building with arched windows and double doors.

Our tour guide met us in the lobby. "Welcome to the Ryman, also known as the Mother Church of Country Music!" our guide said. "There's a reason this place looks so much like a church—it used to *be* one. And ever since it was converted to an auditorium in the early twentieth century, nearly every star in the history of American country music has played here." She continued narrating the building's past as we followed her upstairs and into a small dressing room. A white leather chair sat in front of a mirror lined in bright lights. On the walls hung photos of stars like Dolly Parton and Tammy Wynette.

"This is the Women of Country dressing room," said the guide. "It was named in honor of the Ryman's best female performers, and it still gets a lot of use today. Just last week, Belle Starr got ready before her show right in that very chair."

One of my classmates squealed in excitement. Even Holliday Hayes looked impressed.

"We've heard of Belle Starr," Ms. Carter said, smiling.

"One of my coworkers met her," the guide said. She leaned in and lowered her voice as if she was about to tell us a secret. "She said that Belle was talking all about how just a few years ago she was only playing at family potlucks and her uncle's barbecue restaurant. She could hardly believe that she was playing at the Ryman!"

*I bet **Belle's** parents would have let her play the showcase,* I thought as we trooped through the other rooms and back downstairs.

"I've got one more treat for you," said the tour guide as we turned down a hallway. "Not everyone who visits gets a chance to do this, but your teacher mentioned there were some big music fans here."

We turned another corner. Ahead, some curtains were drawn open next to a sign reading STAGE.

"Y'all ready for your star turn?" the tour guide said, winking.

My heart bounced into my throat. We were
going to stand on the Ryman stage!

We lined up with Ms. Carter in the wings
and peered out into the auditorium. Stunned by
the beauty of the room, I felt my disappointment
about the showcase and my parents fall away.
Light streamed through stained-glass windows
onto rows of wooden pews and the balcony above.
Powerful stage lights shone down onto the wide
stage, which had been polished smooth as glass.
The guide signaled to someone standing at the
back of the auditorium. Suddenly, the stage lights
faded to a single spotlight on an old-fashioned
silver microphone at center stage.

One by one, each of my classmates went onstage
and stood in the spotlight behind the microphone.

When it was Jaya's turn, she struck a rock-star
pose and pulled the microphone to her face. "Hello,
Nashville!" she said, her voice echoing throughout
the theater.

Finally, it was my turn. The air felt cool as I
walked through the shadows, but when I stepped
into the spotlight, it was like standing under a giant

sun. Everything was bright orange until my eyes adjusted.

The audience was a dark sea in front of me. I tilted my face up to the microphone, picturing rows full of people with eager faces, waiting to hear my songs. Electric wonder buzzed through me. I could barely feel the stage under my feet. *I wonder if this was what Belle Starr felt when she performed here*, I thought. *And Patsy Cline! And Taylor Swift!* I imagined singing into the gleaming microphone, my voice ringing out strong and clear, the audience singing along with every word.

"Tenney?" A hand tapped me on the shoulder. Ms. Carter stood behind me, smiling. "Honey, I've been calling your name."

From the darkness, I heard kids snickering.

"Sorry," I said, embarrassed.

As my eyes readjusted to the dark of the theater, I took one last look at the view from the Ryman stage, memorizing it. *Someday I'll come back here to perform*, I promised myself.

My brain buzzed during the whole ride back to
school. Standing on the Ryman stage had inspired
me. *Who cares if I can't play the showcase?* I thought.
*The important thing is to write great songs and perform
them whenever I can.* "You look like you're in a better
mood," Jaya said with a nudge.

I grinned, feeling energized. "Belle Starr played
potlucks and barbecues, anywhere she could. That's
what *I* need to do—starting with the Jamboree."

"Yes!" Jaya said. "Have you signed up yet?"

I shook my head, suddenly remembering that
Ms. Carter had urged us to sign up before it was too
late. "What if all the slots are already full?"

"They won't be," Jaya replied, but her voice was
uncertain.

When the bus dropped us off at Magnolia
Hills, we raced to Ms. Carter's classroom. The
sign-up sheet was still on the door. Every line had
someone's name on it . . . except for the last one.

"Thank goodness!" I said. I wrote my name
down. Under "talent/act" I wrote *singer-songwriter.*

"I'm so excited to hear your song!" Jaya said,
clapping.

"Me, too," I said. "Now I just have to finish it!"

"*You* write songs?" came a voice from behind me. Holliday Hayes was standing there, looking like she'd just eaten something rotten.

"Yeah," I said, "and I play guitar and sing."

"Tenney's amazing," chirped Jaya.

Holliday made an angry noise, like a cough and a snort mixed together. "Congratulations," she said.

Before I could reply, she brushed by us down the hall.

"What's wrong with her?" Jaya asked.

"I don't know," I said, confused. I didn't have time to worry about her, though. I was thinking about what Mom had said: A music career doesn't just take talent—it takes hard work. I needed to find the words to my song.

A BREAKTHROUGH

Chapter 10

*M*om and Dad worked late that night, so Mason cooked dinner. The frozen pizza was burned and the peas were shriveled, but I ate everything as fast as possible. I finished my homework and then carried my guitar and journal into the family room to work on my new song.

Aubrey followed me into the room with a handful of markers and a notepad.

"Aubrey, I'm working," I said to her.

"I'll be quiet, I promise," she said, kneeling on the floor in front of the coffee table to spread out her supplies.

I turned to a blank page in my journal and tried to focus. *I haven't liked any of the lyrics I've come up with so far,* I thought. *So I'll start from scratch.* Shifting my guitar into place, I played the melody slowly. Every now and then, I'd stop and write down ideas for lyrics as they came to me. When I was done, I looked at my brainstorming page. *Love, miss, night, stars* . . . Words spiraled around one another like dragonflies. Each of my verses had five lines, so I tried making up short sentences, singing them as I played. I rhymed "night" with "flight," but the phrases didn't seem to go anywhere. I finally found a couple of verses that made sense and matched the melody. But when I sang them, they sounded forced and hollow.

Mason stuck his head into the family room. "Time for bed, Aubrey."

"Five more minutes," she said, pouting. But before she could protest more, Mason scooped her up and tickled her until they were both laughing.

"Shh, I'm trying to write!" I said, but Aubrey's giggles were so infectious I couldn't help laughing along.

"C'mon, Aubrey," Mason said. "Let's go upstairs to give Queen Tenney some peace and quiet." He winked at me and threw Aubrey over his shoulder.

"That song had better be about *me!*" Aubrey

shouted as Mason carried her upstairs.

I smiled and let my eyes wander to Aubrey's drawing. She'd drawn our family: Mom held a whisk and bowl, Dad led Waylon on his leash, Mason banged on a snare drum, Aubrey posed like a ballerina, and I played my guitar.

I put the drawing on the kitchen table for Mom and Dad, and looked out the window at the night sky, starry over our backyard. Waylon sat on the porch, eyelids drooping. *Maybe I just need a change of scene*, I thought. I grabbed my guitar and journal and headed outside to Waylon's doghouse. From where I sat in the dark, I could see the kitchen lit from within. *Okay, new approach*, I thought. *Ask questions.*

What's the song about?

Love.

What about it?

Um . . .

I had no idea what I wanted to say about love. That it was good? That it made me happy? That seemed obvious. I remembered what Portia had told me: *A good song is always about something meaningful to you.*

A BREAKTHROUGH

Okay, I thought, *so this song is about someone I love. But who?* I'd never been in love or had my heart broken, but all my favorite songs were about losing something the songwriter loved. I couldn't think of anything I'd lost besides my favorite hat, and that didn't seem important enough to write a whole song about. But I couldn't think of anything else. I was stuck. My heart felt like a crumpled-up piece of paper. I yawned and rubbed my eyes, but I didn't want to go to sleep without having written at least one good lyric for this song.

Then I heard the low rumble of Mom's food truck backing into the driveway. Mom parked and got out. I almost called out to her, but then I saw her face; her eyes were puffy and tired and her mouth was drawn into a weary frown. I'd never seen her look so exhausted. Usually, I was asleep when she got home from work. She trudged up the back porch steps, entered the kitchen, and sank into a chair at the table.

Suddenly, a smile warmed her face, and I saw her pick up Aubrey's drawing. She studied it for a long time, her eyes bright with love.

I took in a sharp breath, realizing that I knew what my song was about. I wrote down a title in my journal: "Reach the Sky." Exhilarated, I started writing, the words flooding out of me. I wrote down all the things I wanted to tell Mom in that moment. I stopped worrying about writing the perfect song and just let my thoughts flow.

By bedtime, I'd finished a rough draft of the song lyrics. I sang it to myself, softly. It wasn't perfect, but I loved it. I'd said what I wanted to say. For the first time maybe in forever, I felt like song-writing was what I was born to do.

A STRONGER BRIDGE

Chapter 11

"*W*hen are you going to play me your new song?" Jaya asked the next day at lunch.

"When it's ready," I replied. "It still needs work. But maybe you'll get to hear it at the Jamboree!" Even if "Reach the Sky" wasn't perfect yet, I thought, it was a solid start.

Jaya wrinkled her nose at me across the lunchroom table and bit into her peanut butter and jelly sandwich. "Speaking of the Jamboree, have you and Portia figured out what activity you're doing as a team?"

I shook my head. "Portia didn't seem too excited about the Jamboree, actually."

"What *is* she excited about?" Jaya asked.

"Well, she likes music—" Before I'd even finished my sentence, an idea hit me like a bolt of lightning. I drew in a sharp breath. "I should ask her to perform a duet with me at the Jamboree!" I blurted. "She plays guitar. I bet she sings, too. How come I didn't think of that before?"

"I have no idea," Jaya said, and we both laughed.

After school, we headed to the senior center with Ms. Carter and the rest of the kids on the Jamboree committee. As soon as we arrived, I started looking for Portia. I didn't see her at first, but I eventually found her tucked into a corner of the small study where I'd played her guitar.

"Well, if it isn't Miss Tenney," Portia said as I walked up. "What brings you a-calling?"

I hesitated. The last two times I'd visited, Portia hadn't wanted to talk about the Jamboree. She'd liked hearing my song, though. Maybe if I played her the version with lyrics, she'd like it enough to agree to perform with me at the Jamboree.

"I finished my song," I said. "Will you listen to it and let me know what you think?"

Interest flickered in Portia's eyes. She nodded.

A STRONGER BRIDGE

My stomach did a nervous wiggle as I picked up her guitar. I hadn't played the song for anyone yet. I wanted an honest opinion, though, and I had a feeling that Portia wasn't going to hold back just because I was a kid.

"Whenever you're ready," Portia said.

I started playing, keeping my eyes on the guitar. I was worried I'd forget the words if I looked at Portia. By the second verse, though, I was relaxed enough to glance up at her. She was listening carefully, but I couldn't tell what she thought, even after the song ended.

After a long pause, she finally spoke. "It's good. Better than good, actually."

"Thanks," I said, feeling pleased.

"Don't get too excited; it's not a home run—yet," she said. "I have some suggestions if you're interested."

She put out her hands, and I gave her the guitar. Then Portia did something incredible: She started *playing* my song, note for note. I couldn't believe what a great guitar player she was. She'd only seen me play the melody twice!

"The verse and the chorus are catchy," she said, breezing through the melody, "but the bridge could be bigger. Maybe something like this?"

She improvised on my bridge, picking up the tempo. "This song has fire," she said. "You need to bring that out more."

"You're *really* good," I said. I watched in awe as her fingers danced over the guitar's frets.

Portia chuckled. When she started playing faster, though, her chord hand jittered. Before I could blink, it shuddered again. The music turned into a muddle. Portia yanked up her hand, clenching it into a tight fist.

"Are you okay?" I asked.

"Not really," she said. She laid the guitar in her lap.

"What happened to your hand?" I asked softly.

"Six months ago, I had a stroke," Portia said. "I'm doing much better now, but the muscles in this hand are still very weak." She looked at her hands as if she was embarrassed.

"You shouldn't feel bad," I said. "You're still a great guitar player. You just need to practice."

"I know," she said.

"Maybe I could come back with my guitar and we could practice together," I said.

Portia squinted at me for a long while. "Maybe. Okay," she said finally.

"Um, also, I signed up to perform at the Jamboree," I told her. "I'm pretty nervous about it."

"Well, you don't get better by going around what you're scared of," Portia said.

"Maybe I wouldn't be so nervous if you performed with me . . ." I said.

"I don't think so," Portia said.

"Why not?" I pushed. "You're a great player, and we need to do something together for the Jamboree. I think it would be fun."

"No," Portia snapped.

I shut my mouth and looked at her, unsure what else to say.

Portia's eyes softened a little. "Sorry," she said, "but I don't perform anymore."

"I thought you don't get better by going around what you're scared of," I replied.

Portia pressed her mouth into a stiff, stubborn

line, and shrugged. "What else can we do at the Jamboree?"

"I guess we could work the bake sale table..." I fumbled.

"Fine," Portia said. And as she gazed out the window, I knew the conversation was over.

That night, I worked on "Reach the Sky." First, I made up a stronger bridge, as Portia had suggested. Then I polished the lyrics, double-checking every word to make sure it was the one I wanted. The song felt stronger, but I wanted to bounce it off someone whose ear I trusted, and I wasn't going to see Portia again until later in the week. So I went to the garage to find my brother.

Mason was at his worktable soldering wires. When he saw me, he jumped up, pulling off his safety goggles. "I'm in the middle of something!" he huffed.

"Sor-ry!" I said. "I just need five minutes to play you a song."

A STRONGER BRIDGE

"Oh! Why didn't you say so?" Mason said, grinning. He tossed a towel over his project and sat back. "Go for it."

I took a deep breath and started playing. I jumbled a few new words, but I thought I played okay. When I was done, though, Mason stared at me like I had three heads.

"You *wrote* that?" he asked.

"Yeah," I said defensively. "Why?"

"Tenney, that song's good enough to be on the radio!" Mason said.

"Really?" I said, my heart soaring.

"Yes!" Mason said. "You need to go play that for Mom and Dad right now. It's awesome!" He started for the door.

"Wait!" I said. "I don't want to play it for them yet."

"Why not?" Mason asked. "Tenney, this song proves you're a *real* songwriter."

Joy flooded into me. I'd been waiting forever to hear someone say that. "Thank you," I mumbled.

"Don't thank me, *believe* me," Mason said. His eyes were serious.

"I want Mom and Dad to hear the song at the Jamboree, when I've really got it down. I just wish I had more opportunities to perform it first," I said, thinking out loud, "so I could get used to playing solo in front of people. But there's no way."

Mason drummed his fingers on his desk, thinking.

"Maybe there is," he said.

"What do you mean? The Tri-Stars don't have another show until next month, and we already know that the showcase isn't happening."

Mason started to reply, then stopped himself. "I'll get back to you on that," he told me.

PRINTERS ALLEY

Chapter 12

𝓜ason's words were a distant memory when Jaya bounced up to my locker a few days later. She seemed way too happy considering how much homework we had for the weekend.

"What are you doing after school?" she asked, her eyes sparkling with mischief.

I shrugged. "I guess I'll get a head start on my book report."

Jaya shook her head. "I have a better idea ..."

I wasn't sure what she was talking about— until we walked out of school and found my brother leaning against Dad's truck by the front steps.

"You weren't supposed to pick me up today," I said, confused.

"I had to," Mason said with a grin. "It's a special occasion."

He pulled down the door of the truck bed.
Inside was my guitar case and the broken amplifier
that Mason had taken from Dad's shop. *Tenney
Grant* was splashed across the front of the amp,
painted in Jaya's curvy, unique font, and pretty
pink flowers danced along the sides.

I looked from Jaya to Mason, stunned. "I don't
understand," I said.

"We fixed it up for you!" Jaya said.

"Every great musician needs an amp. How else
are people going to hear you when you perform
today?" Mason said with a twinkle in his eye.

"Wait—today?" I squeaked.

"Yup!" he replied. "Nashville needs to hear
Tenney Grant's music right now, don't you think?"

I gulped. This was happening really fast. Even
so, I was more thrilled than afraid. Excitement
pulsed through me.

"Yes!" I said at last. It was now or never.

Fifteen minutes later, the three of us were riding
down Broadway, the crowded heart of Nashville's
music scene. I pressed my nose to the window. Bright
neon signs for Tootsie's Orchid Lounge and Robert's

Western World blinked as we passed by, and I could hear the echo of live music booming through their open doors. *Legendary musicians play these clubs*, I thought with a shiver. Even being in the same neighborhood was intimidating. I wondered whether Dad would ever book the Tri-Stars at one of these venues.

My breath caught in my chest as I remembered how my parents said I was too young to perform.

"Mason, you checked with Mom and Dad about doing this, right?" I asked.

"They said it was fine to take you and Jaya downtown," Mason said without taking his eyes off the road. "Help me look for parking."

"Okay," I said, feeling a rush of relief.

We found parking off Commerce Street and got out of the car.

"I'm not sure I should try to play on Broadway," I said, as Mason unloaded the gear.

"I couldn't have gotten you a slot at one of these clubs anyway," Mason admitted, handing me my guitar. "So how about Printers Alley?"

"Yes!" I said. "That's perfect!"

Downtown Nashville has a bunch of quaint

alleys and side streets, and Printers Alley is the
most famous one. A hundred years ago it was the
booming center of the printing trade in Tennessee.
The print shops are long gone, but there's still a
gorgeous old sign reading PRINTERS ALLEY over the
entrance. It's a popular photo spot for tourists.

As we lugged the gear over to Church Street,
I started to get nervous.

"Where will we plug in the amp?" I asked.
"It's okay if I have to play without the speaker."
Maybe it's better if people can't hear me, I thought
to myself.

Mason explained that he had rewired the amp
to run on batteries. "It's portable," he said proudly.
"The mic hooks up to the amp, too."

"Don't worry, Tenney," said Jaya. "You'll be
loud enough that they'll hear you all the way up the
block!"

"Great," I said, even though the idea set my
heart racing.

We reached Printers Alley and found a cool
mural inside the lane where there was space to set
up. Mason showed me how to use the amp's foot

pedal to start an electronic backbeat.

"It's like your drummer," he said. "It'll help keep time while you play. You ready?" He plugged in my guitar's pickup and then switched on the amp and the microphone.

I nodded, but I didn't know how to start. Standing awkwardly on the edge of the sidewalk, I felt invisible. People hurried past me, paying no attention to me and my guitar.

What if no one stops to listen to me? I thought. *Or what if they do—and they hate my song?* My stomach shrank into a worried ball. I put my fingers on the guitar strings, but my hands were trembling.

"I'm Tenney Grant," I tried to say, but all that came out was a dry choke. I may not have been on a real stage, but I had big-time stage fright.

I looked over. Mason's and Jaya's faces were creased with concern.

Pull yourself together, I told myself. I took a deep breath to shake off my nerves. It didn't help. I stood there, frozen.

Finally, Mason came over. He switched off the microphone.

"You okay?" he asked.

"No," I said miserably. "Maybe this wasn't such a good idea."

"Tenney, if you want to be a singer, you have to *sing*," Mason said gently.

"I don't know how to start," I said, my voice small.

"You want some help?" Mason asked.

I nodded, moving back from the mic.

Mason stepped forward. "As soon as I finish," he murmured to me, "you start in with 'Carolina Highway.' You know that song forward and backward, so it should feel really natural."

"Okay," I said, wiping my palms on my jeans.

"Ladies and gentlemen, can I have your attention, please!" Mason shouted, spreading his arms like an old-time announcer. All he needed was a tuxedo. "Y'all ready to hear some great music? Are you?" he said to a passing couple.

They laughed and slowed down.

"Well, you're in luck!" Mason continued. "Because I'm offering you front-row seats to see one of the most talented twelve-year-olds in the country! So stop right here but step on back, because Tenney Grant is about to ROCK. THIS. STREET!"

He slid sideways, and I pushed up to the mic, diving into the intro for "Carolina Highway." As my hands flew, I laughed, giving in to the joy of playing fast. Right as the lyrics were about to kick in, I closed my eyes. It helped me focus. I could listen to my voice and control my breathing better.

"This Carolina highway's full of dead ends and byways," I sang. *"This Carolina highway's awfully dark."*

By the middle of the song, I felt relaxed enough to open my eyes. My audience had grown to around a dozen people! Seeing them gave me a jolt of energy.

I put everything I had into the rest of the song. When I finished, the crowd broke into applause. I blushed and gave a little curtsy. When I looked up, I spotted our next-door neighbor Ms. Pavone across the street. She gave me a big thumbs-up, adjusted her enormous purple glasses, and turned to continue up the street.

I grinned and started talking before I could get nervous again. "This next song is a brand-new one.

It's called 'Reach the Sky,'" I said.

This time, I forced myself to look at the crowd as I strummed the first chords. I imagined Mom in the front row, watching me. The crowd smiled back at me, tapping their feet and swaying in time to *my* song. It felt like a dream.

"I am planted in the ground, tiny like a seed," I sang. *"Someday I will make you proud. I'll be steady like a tree."*

I finished the first verse, then the second. With each line, I told Mom that I loved her in my mind. And then, all at once, the song was over and the crowd cheered. I felt a wave of joy wash over me. I never wanted this moment to end.

Mason and Jaya couldn't stop raving about my performance on the way home.

"You were on fire, Tenney!" said Jaya.

Mason agreed. "That was your best performance ever!"

I beamed. I felt like a floating balloon, buoyed

by happiness. "That was so amazing!" I said.
"I can't wait to tell Mom and Dad how it went!"

Suddenly, Mason's smile disappeared and he grew quiet. I knew something was wrong. "The thing is, Tenney . . . they kind of didn't know you were performing," he admitted.

"What?!" Jaya and I said at once.

Joy melted into worry in my stomach.

"But you told me Mom and Dad said it was okay!" I huffed, throwing an outraged glare at Mason.

"No, I said that we had permission to go *downtown*," Mason corrected me. "There's no way they would have let you perform if I'd asked; they're way too protective."

"How could you not *tell* me?" I protested.

"Because you never would have performed, and you *needed* to," said Mason. "Besides, Mom and Dad don't ever have to find out about this."

I gulped when an image of big purple glasses flashed in my head. "Actually . . ."

Mason looked at me. "What?"

I told him about seeing Ms. Pavone during my

performance. "Mason, we *have* to tell them."

My brother gritted his teeth. "Fine. But if Mom and Dad are upset about you performing, that's their problem, not yours."

I frowned. I wasn't so sure Mason was right. But I was sure of one thing: If my parents found out about Printers Alley from Ms. Pavone—and not from us—they'd never let me perform again.

"Tenney, aren't you hungry?" Mom said, wrinkling her brow at me from across the kitchen table at dinner.

"Oh, yeah," I said, taking a bite of chili. But I didn't really have an appetite. My head was swimming with worry. *I want to have a music career,* I thought. *But I'll never get to be a real musician if I don't get to perform more. I need Mom and Dad's support. I need to tell them how I'm feeling—without getting Mason in trouble.*

"Mom, Dad," I said at last, "I'd like permission to perform more."

Maybe if I get their permission now, I thought, *they won't mind that I already performed today.*

Mom and Dad exchanged a look.

"You're playing the Jamboree in a few weeks," Mom pointed out.

"And the Tri-Stars have a gig at the library fund-raiser next month," Dad added, reaching for another roll. "We'll need you to keep singing lead on a couple of songs, and we can start rehearsing them that way this weekend." He gave me a wink.

"That's great, Dad, thanks," I said. "But I want to try to play more solo shows."

Before my parents could say no, I rushed on. "Look, I love performing, and I've been working on my songs," I said. "I know you guys don't want me to play the Mockingbird Records showcase, but even if I don't, I still want to perform more, at *real* shows."

"Honey, we've been over this," Mom said firmly. "You're too young, and that's the way it is."

"Yeah," Aubrey said.

"Aubrey, don't pile on," Mom said, giving her a gentle warning glance.

My whole chest throbbed with anger and hurt,

but I tried to stay calm. I turned to my brother, silently pleading with him to back me up.

Mason cleared his throat. "You guys should hear Tenney's new song. It's fantastic. Good enough to record!"

Mom took a bite of salad and nodded.

"I'm not kidding," Mason said to her.

"I know you're not," Mom said.

Mom reached over and put her hand on mine. "Tenney, I know you want to be a singer-songwriter, but—"

"No, Mom, I *am* a singer-songwriter!" I said sharply. "When I performed my song today, people loved it!"

Mom blinked about five hundred times in one second. "W-wait. Today? Where did you perform?" she asked.

I hesitated. Mason was begging me with his eyes not to say anything, but I had to be honest.

"Printers Alley," I said. "But Mason and Jaya were with me the whole time. We were totally safe!"

Dad's face went beet red. Mason looked like he wanted to crawl under the table.

"I was *good*. You can ask Mason and Jaya,"
I insisted, plunging into my argument. "I know you
want me to wait until I'm older, but I'm good at this
right *now*. And I want to get better! But I can't do
that if I don't perform."

"We've heard enough," Dad said.

"You both knew you needed permission before
doing any sort of performance," Mom said. "There-
fore, you're both grounded until further notice."

"Don't punish Tenney," Mason said. "She
thought we had permission."

"She should have known better," Dad said.

I stared at my glass, trying not to cry. It didn't
work. I rushed out of the kitchen, hot tears stinging
my eyes. As I ran upstairs, I couldn't escape this
horrible feeling in the pit of my stomach that my
life was over.

A SECOND CHANCE

Chapter 13

*A*s soon as I got to my room, I curled on my
bed and cried. Fat drops of disappointment
slipped down my cheeks. I wiped them away. I
hate crying, even if it does make me feel better
sometimes.

I picked up the jar full of guitar picks from my
nightstand. I began collecting picks after my first
guitar lesson at Dad's shop. For a while, everyone
in my family was adding to my collection whenever they found one. I had picks from music stores
and guitar makers, and ones advertising artists
and records. Usually, looking at them reminded
me of how many people music touches. Right now,
though, they just made me sad. So did the framed
78 rpm record of "Hound Dog" over my bed that
Mom gave me for my eighth birthday.

A SECOND CHANCE

Why did my parents teach me to play music if they weren't going to let me perform? I wondered. I sat up and wiped the tears from my cheeks. *Don't just feel bad,* I told myself. *Do something.*

I scrambled to the end of my bed and hauled up my beater guitar. I wrapped myself around it and picked out a melody that was sad and angry and dramatic, everything I was feeling at that moment. As I played, I felt my emotions flowing into the guitar, as if the music was expressing all the things I couldn't say. I'd been playing for a few minutes when Aubrey opened the door. She glared at me and crossed the room to her dresser.

"Mom and Dad are fighting, so good job," she said, pulling out her pajamas.

I didn't say anything. Through the floor, I could hear the muffled sound of my parents' angry voices downstairs.

"You shouldn't have lied to them," Aubrey said.

"I didn't *lie*," I replied hotly. My mouth trembled, like I could cry again. "I was honest. I just want a chance to perform my music."

I rubbed my face to stop the tears. When I

looked back, Aubrey's eyes were lowered to the floor, and I could tell that she felt bad for making me cry.

"If it were up to me, I would let you play," she said. "Your songs are really good."

"Thanks," I said hopelessly.

Aubrey hugged me and got into her bed.

There was no way I could sleep right now, so I took my guitar and left, shutting off the light as I went.

As I tiptoed downstairs, I could hear my parents talking in the family room, their voices much calmer than they had been a half hour ago.

Mom sighed. "Ray, you know what the music business can do to people."

"Tenney has us to protect her, Georgia," Dad said. "We can guide her and support her—and if we have to, we can say no down the line. All I'm saying is maybe our decision is too extreme. Playing the showcase doesn't mean she has to chase a professional career."

Part of me wanted to keep eavesdropping, but I didn't want my parents to catch me. I slipped through the kitchen and quietly stepped out the porch door. Waylon ambled over as I sat down on the porch steps and looked out at the yard, trying to leave this miserable day behind. The night was cool and quiet. I watched a glimmering dragonfly flitting over the grass.

I shifted my guitar to my knees. Resting my fingers on the strings, I replayed the song I'd started in my room, this time a bit slower and softer.

"*La-la-la-la*," I sang. "*Laa-la-la.*"

Behind me, the door whispered open. I stopped playing and looked over my shoulder. Mom was watching me from the doorway.

"Sorry," she said. "I didn't mean to startle you."

"It's okay," I said. "I was just fooling around with an idea."

Mom sat down by me and scratched Waylon behind his ears. "Will you play me something?" she asked.

I hesitated. I still felt very hurt, but I wanted to play for her so badly. I took a deep breath and started "Reach the Sky." Halfway through the intro, I looked over at Mom. She was watching me intently with a gentle smile. A wave of shyness hit me. I looked into the yard, at the green grass and the dancing dragonfly, and started singing.

> *I am planted in the ground*
> *Tiny like a seed*
> *Someday I will make you proud*
> *I'll be steady like a tree*
> *Will you teach me how to grow?*
>
> *Gonna be myself, nobody else*
> *Gonna reach the sky if I only try*
>
> *I admit that I am young*
> *Tucked beneath your wings*
> *But someday I'll be on my own*
> *Wild and flying free*
> *Will you teach me how to sing?*
>
> *Gonna be myself, nobody else*
> *Gonna reach the sky if I only try*

A SECOND CHANCE

I sent the song into the cool night air, feeling every word. I stumbled twice on the tough part of the bridge, but I kept going.

> *I know you wanna keep me*
> *Safe away at home*
> *But I've got my own dreams*
> *And I can't tell them no*

> *Gonna be myself, nobody else*
> *Gonna reach the sky if I only try*

I didn't look at Mom until I finished. Her eyes were wet with tears.

"Why are you sad?" I said, alarmed.

"I'm not sad—I'm proud of you," she said, wiping her eyes. "Your song is fantastic, Tenney. I can tell it's really meaningful to you."

I almost told Mom that she inspired the song, but I didn't want her to think that was why I'd sung it. I did want her to know how I felt, though.

"I know you and Dad are trying to do what's best for me," I told her, "but I can't help what I feel.

I want to perform more than anything else in the world."

Mom nodded and thought for a long while.

"Honey, a music career takes time and sacrifice, and nothing's fair about the business," she said. "A lot of pain in my life has come from that fact."

"What do you mean?" I asked. "Tell me what happened."

Mom's jaw flexed. I could tell she was wrestling with how to say what she needed to tell me.

"My momma had really high hopes for me when I was your age," she said finally. "She was convinced I was going to be a big star, and she wanted that more than anything."

"And you *didn't* want that?" I said.

Mom gave me a bittersweet smile. "I was like you. I wanted to write songs and share them with people who loved music as much as I did," she said. "But my mom wanted more for me. So she pushed me really hard. She took me to see some producers when I turned sixteen, and this producer wanted to sign me. He paid us a few thousand dollars to record a single."

"Your demo?"

"Yes," Mom replied, "except when we got in the studio, the song I was supposed to record wasn't mine, it was some other song that I didn't like. It wasn't *me*."

"Oh," I said.

"My momma urged me to cut the demo. So I did it," said Mom. "But afterward, I asked the producer about *my* songs. He said we'd have to wait on those—and in the meantime, I'd need to dye my hair blonde, lose ten pounds, and start wearing high heels."

I frowned, confused. "What does any of that have to do with music?"

Mom let out a laugh. "That's what I said!" she replied. "It turned out that for the producer, the music business was more about the *business* than the music. In other words, he just wanted to make money off me, and he thought he'd make more money if I changed who I was."

"So what did you do?" I asked.

"I dyed my hair for about five minutes," Mom said. "It looked pretty bad, but it helped me decide

I'd rather be true to myself. Good thing, too, because the producer decided I wasn't 'star material' after all. That was fine by me, but when I asked for my songs back, he said that the label owned them now."

I gasped.

"Was that true?" I asked.

Mom nodded. "Momma gave him the rights in the contract she signed," she said. "Then it got worse. After I left, I wrote more songs and I got some meetings with other record labels. They all knew who I was. I found out the producer was telling people I was hard to work with, so they didn't want to sign me."

I shook my head. "That's so unfair! How could he even get away with that?"

"I'm not sure he could today," Mom said, "but he was a powerful guy back then."

I squeezed Mom's hand. For the first time, I understood why she had been so worried about me starting in the music business. "I'm really sorry that happened to you," I said.

Mom put an arm around me. "It was years ago, but it took me a long while to get over it. And of course, I don't want something like that to ever happen to you or your music," she said. "At the same time, I see how talented you are. And it's clear that the older you get, the more you love music.

"I know you have been working so hard on your music even though we told you that you couldn't play the showcase." She paused and took a deep breath. "I've thought about it a lot, and it seems unfair to stand in your way just because I'm afraid that you might face disappointment or pain in a music career. If I keep you from doing what you love, you'll blame me—and you'll be right," Mom continued. "Your dad also reminded me that we can help make sure you and your music are more protected than I was."

I nodded, but I was still confused. "So what are you saying? Am I still grounded?"

Mom gave me a warm smile. "I think you and Mason have learned your lesson, and we're glad you told us the truth. But we don't want you to go sneaking around to perform again. So what I'm really saying is that Dad and I have decided that we'll allow you to perform at the Mockingbird

Records showcase—as long as you promise to take it slow and not let performing get in the way of what matters most: your family, your friends, and your schoolwork."

Shocked, I tried to speak, but all that came out was a squeak. I threw my arms around her.

"I hope that's a good noise," she said with a chuckle.

"I promise I'll make you proud," I said.

She clasped my face in her hands. "You already have."

NOTHING SPECIAL

Chapter 14

*T*hat weekend, I only put down my guitar long
enough to eat, sleep, and do homework. By
Sunday evening, my fingers were raw from playing.
I had a backache and I was tired, but I was starting
to feel prepared.

As I shuffled up to my locker on Monday, Jaya
gave me a concerned once-over.

"You look like you just saw ten Taylor Swift
shows back-to-back," she said. "Were your parents
super mad about Printers Alley?"

"Oh my gosh! I was so busy practicing that I
forgot to call you." I told her everything, from being
grounded to playing my song for Mom to finding
out I could play the showcase.

"No *way*," Jaya said.

"It's true!" Though I could hardly believe it

myself. "This could be my only chance to ever play at the Bluebird. I have to be really good," I said as we entered the girls' restroom.

Jaya put her hands on my shoulders. "Tenney, you got invited to perform at a professional show-case at the Bluebird Cafe hosted by Mockingbird Records! I'd say you're *already* good. What if they give you a record contract?!"

"Everyone performing at the showcase will be hoping for that," I said.

"They're not Tenney Grant," Jaya said, grinning.

I smiled back. Jaya's confidence in me always makes me feel like I can do anything.

A stall clicked open behind us. Holliday Hayes sailed over to a sink, glancing at me in the mirror. A snicker slipped out of her.

"What's so funny?" Jaya asked, bristling.

"Nothing," Holliday shrugged. "I just think it's silly to think Tenney would have a chance at a record deal, that's all."

"What do you know?" Jaya fired back. "You've never even heard Tenney sing."

Holliday shrugged, and when she looked at

me, her blue eyes sparkled like hard, cold jewels.
"My dad *runs* a record label, remember?" she said.
"I know how hard it is to make it big in music.
You're Tenney Grant, not Taylor Swift. You're nothing special. I'm sure your music won't be, either."

My face was on fire, but I kept my voice steady
when I replied. "I'm just going to play my music
and do my best."

"Good luck," said Holliday, but the edge in her
voice made it clear that she didn't mean it at all. She
pushed past us and out the bathroom door.

I stood perfectly still, feeling as if Holliday had
trampled my heart with her plaid high-tops.

Jaya stepped in front of me, her eyes burning.
"Tenney, don't listen to one stupid word Holliday
said. You are the one and only Tennyson Evangeline
Grant. And you're going to be amazing."

As Jaya hugged me, I tried to believe that.

BACKFLIPS & BUTTERFLIES

Chapter 15

*T*he morning of the showcase, I woke up to the smell of fresh blueberry muffins.

Suddenly I remembered: *Tonight I'm singing at the Bluebird Cafe!* A storm of excitement flooded through me. Then I heard Holliday's words echoing in my mind: *You're nothing special. I'm sure your music won't be, either.*

Was Holliday right? What if my performance totally bombed? What if I did great, but nobody liked my song?

I've got to practice, I decided. So I shook off my worry and bounded downstairs and into the kitchen.

"You're up early," Mom said, rinsing a sudsy spatula at the sink. "The muffins will be ready in a few minutes."

I kissed her good morning. "Thanks, but I'm too nervous to eat right now. I'm going to go practice for a little while."

Mom nodded sympathetically. "Just be sure to play quietly so you don't wake up Aubrey and Mason."

I headed for the family room and grabbed my guitar from its stand before sitting cross-legged in front of the couch. Taking a deep breath to calm my jitters, I started playing scales to warm up. Within a few minutes, my stomach and my mind had settled down.

For the next hour, I played "Reach the Sky" nonstop. I practiced the chord progressions and worked on the parts where I sometimes mess up. Finally, Mom brought me a muffin and convinced me to take a break.

Dad poked his head in from the kitchen. "Thank goodness you stopped playing," he said.

"Why?" I asked, confused.

"Because I have something better for you to practice on," he said. He stepped into the room with a guitar case in his hand.

"What is that?" I said.

Dad gave me a lopsided grin and set the case in front of me. I ran my fingers over its smooth leather surface. Its shiny brass snap locks looked like they'd never been touched.

"Go ahead, open it," Dad said.

I flipped open the clasps, lifted the lid, and gasped. It was my favorite mini Taylor guitar from my dad's store, glowing aquamarine against the pink velvet of the case's interior and leaving me breathless.

"Dad, this is too nice for me," I said.

"You're playing a professional gig," Mom said, putting her arm around Dad's waist. "So you need a professional guitar. Go on, try it out."

I picked it up and strummed the first chords of my song. It sounded cleaner and clearer, richer and deeper than it had on my beater guitar. Playing it made me feel like I could fly.

"It's amazing," I said, hugging my parents. "Thank you so much."

"This is an incredible opportunity for you as an artist, Tenney," Dad said seriously. "Who knows who could be listening at the Bluebird tonight."

"I know," I said. Once again my stomach twisted into a nervous pretzel. A professional guitar meant I had no excuse for sounding bad onstage.

For the next few hours, I rehearsed with my new guitar on the porch. I'd played it before, of course, but *performing* with a new instrument is different. The strings were tighter than they'd been on my old beater, and I had to adjust the position of my left hand to get it around the guitar's wider neck.

Maybe I shouldn't play it at the show, I thought, but quickly dismissed that idea. My parents had given me my dream guitar. I *had* to play it.

As the day wore on, I tried to keep myself busy by reading and helping Mom in the kitchen and playing with Aubrey, but I couldn't focus. The showcase was in just a couple of hours, and it was all I could think about.

"Earth to Tenney," Aubrey said, waving her

hands in front of my face. "It's your turn."

I looked down at our tic-tac-toe game and saw that her Xs had me trapped. "You win," I said. "What should we do now?"

Aubrey perked up, her eyes sparkling with an idea. "Let's get ready for your showcase!" she said.

I'd thought about performing for weeks, but somehow I hadn't considered what to wear. As soon as we got upstairs, though, it became clear that Aubrey had spent *a lot* of time thinking about it. Within minutes, she'd laid out some outfits for me to try on: a pink dress with puffy sleeves and one of Aubrey's tiaras, a super-fancy sequined dress that I used to wear when Jaya and I played dress-up, and a paisley lace top and sparkly tulle skirt.

"You have to try this one," Aubrey insisted, holding up the pink dress. It was her style, not mine. It was itchy and frilly, and I'd hated wearing it to my cousin's baptism last year. Luckily, it was too small now. And the sequined dress was fraying and way too showy. So that left the lace top and sparkly tulle skirt. Mom had bought them for me hoping I'd wear them for a Tri-Stars performance, but it always seemed too fancy for our shows at East Park and the library parking lot. I twirled around, looking at myself in the mirror. It was perfect for the showcase.

Aubrey squinted at me. "It needs something."

"Like what?" I asked warily. I was *not* going to wear her tiara.

"Like this," Aubrey said, holding out a small box wrapped in pink paper. "Open it."

She bounced nervously as I ripped through the paper. Inside the box was a pretty hair comb covered in overlapping guitar picks that had been neatly glued together like tiny feathers.

"Wow! Where did you find this?" I asked.

"I *made* it," Aubrey said. "I've been collecting picks just like you do. Do you like it?"

"I love it!" I said, and hugged her.

"I can't wait to hear you rock out," Aubrey told me, which made me laugh.

"Me, too," said Mom, grinning from the hall-way with a set of hot rollers in her hands.

Aubrey watched as Mom set my long hair in the rollers, then brushed it out in long waves. She fixed Aubrey's comb so it was holding back one side of my hair, then sprayed everything with hairspray. She even let me put on sparkly lip gloss.

"So you don't disappear under the lights," she said, smoothing my hair.

When Aubrey followed Mom downstairs, I hung back, taking one last look in the mirror. I almost didn't recognize myself. With my flowing hair and comb, shimmery makeup and outfit, I looked a little like a movie star.

In an hour, I'll be onstage at the Bluebird.

My stomach clenched, but I inhaled deeply and smiled at the girl in the mirror. *Don't worry,* I said to her in my head. *You're just not used to this yet.*

THE BLUEBIRD CAFE

Chapter 16

*T*he Bluebird Cafe is a small club tucked between shops in a strip mall. If you didn't know that it was one of the most famous music clubs in Nashville, you'd miss it.

Dad pulled into the nearly full parking lot and found a space. The show wasn't starting for another half hour, but the place was already hopping, with people mingling around a handful of tables. A line of microphones stood on a low stage against the back wall, which was lit up with a neon sign of a soaring bluebird and some strings of twinkly lights. The Bluebird wasn't big or fancy like the Ryman Auditorium, but I'd never been more excited to play anywhere.

The host led us to a reserved table by the side of the stage. I sat down facing the club's entrance.

The showcase was by invitation only for performers and guests, and Ellie had told my mom that I could invite my family plus one friend, so I asked Jaya. Before long I spotted her coming through the front door. I caught her eye and waved.

"This place is so cool!" Jaya said, looking around. She unbuttoned her bright green coat, revealing a purple T-shirt with *Tenney Rocks!* printed across it in my special font.

"Great shirt!" I said.

"I made it!" Jaya said. "How else will everybody know that I'm your biggest fan?"

The door opened again, and in walked Ellie Cale with a gray-haired man in a porkpie hat. Ellie grinned at me and led the man to our table.

"Tenney! I'm so glad you're performing tonight," she said.

"Me, too," I said. My voice sounded far off, like I wasn't even in the room.

"Tenney, this is my uncle Zane, the head of Mockingbird Records," Ellie said.

Zane Cale shook my hand and then introduced himself to my family. He didn't really look like the head of a big music label—he looked more like your goofy uncle who plays ukulele. He was wearing red cowboy boots and a bolo tie shaped like the state of Texas. His gray hair stood straight out under his hat, like he'd been electrified, but his eyes were warm and thoughtful as he looked down at me.

"I hear you're twelve," he said solemnly.

"Yes," I replied.

"What sort of music do you like?" he asked.

"A little bit of everything," I said. "But mostly singer-songwriters."

"Well, that's good, because we love singer-songwriters over at Mockingbird," he replied.

"Well, I hope you like my song, Mr. Cale," I said, blushing.

"I hope so, too," he said. "And my friends call me Zane." He gave me a wink and wandered off into the crowd.

"Is he looking to sign new artists?" Mason asked Ellie.

"We're always looking," Ellie said with a sparkle in her eye. She turned back to me and pointed to a row of chairs by the stage where a group of musicians were sitting tuning guitars. "When you're ready, Tenney, you should go sit with the other performers."

I glanced at the group of musicians. Most of them looked at least twenty years old. Ellie gave my shoulder a squeeze and walked off.

Mom glanced at me.

"Are you all right?" she asked, frowning.

I realized I was holding my breath. I nodded, letting out the air in a hard rush. I suddenly felt very warm. Even my feet were sweating. I reached down to loosen the straps on my new shoes.

"I think your cowboy boots are in the truck. Do you want them?" Mom asked.

"Maybe that's a good idea," I said.

I waited by the entrance while Mom went to get my boots. She'd only been gone a moment when the front door opened and Portia walked in wearing a purple poncho and leaning on her carved wood walking stick.

"Portia! What are you doing here?" I cried.

Her face cracked into a big open grin. "A

little bird told me that you were playing here tonight," she said. "And I couldn't miss your big show! Look at you, all fancy."

I smiled. "I'm glad you came." I was about to ask her how she got a ticket for the showcase when she let out a whoop. "This place has more hop than a sack of jackrabbits," she said, laughing.

I giggled and spotted Ellie making her way toward us. I thought she was going to urge me to go sit by the musicians again, but I was surprised when she pulled Portia into a big hug.

"Portia!" she said, beaming. "Aren't you a sight for sore eyes! How are you feeling?"

"Still using this old thing," Portia said, tapping her stick, "but I'm doing better. I came to see Tenney sing," she continued, looking at me.

"I didn't know you knew each other!" Ellie said.

I nodded, but before I had time to ask how *they* knew each other, Ellie hooked her arm with Portia's and said, "Come on with me. Uncle Zane's got a table in back. He'll be so happy you're here."

"All righty," said Portia. She turned to me.

"I'll see you after, Miss Tenney. You knock 'em dead for me."

By the time Mom returned with my boots, the place was so crowded that I couldn't see where Portia and Ellie had gone.

Mom helped me slip on my favorite cowboy boots, and we went back to our table. Dad had my new guitar waiting.

"It's almost five," Dad said, handing it to me. "Time to take your place with the other performers."

This was it. One by one, I hugged everyone. They all wished me luck.

Mom bent down so her face was level with mine. "You're gonna be great," she whispered. "Just be yourself, okay?"

"Okay," I said, and walked over to my seat.

There was one empty chair left, between a girl with cherry-red hair and a short man with sideburns. The next few minutes before the show started seemed to last forever. I tuned my guitar and did vocal warm-ups. As the other performers chatted around me, I caught bits of their conversations.

"I sold the rights to that song, but they wouldn't sign me..."

"...I've been singing backup for Miranda since May to pay the bills."

"I'm supposed to play some clubs in Europe next month..."

The girl beside me warmed up on her banjo, her pick hand hammering out arpeggios at the speed of light.

*These are **real** musicians,* I thought. *And I'm just Tenney Grant.* The butterflies in my stomach stopped twirling and started kickboxing.

Calm down, I thought. I looked around for a distraction. My eyes settled on a RESERVED sign sitting on an empty table right in front of the stage. I took a breath and closed my eyes.

I never should have opened them.

An elegant blonde woman was making her way to the reserved table in front of the stage. Behind her, in perfect lavender cowboy boots, was Holliday Hayes.

Oh no. I wanted to sink through my chair and disappear.

The house lights dimmed and the stage lights came up. Ellie climbed the steps to the microphone.

"Hey, y'all!" she chirped. "Thanks for coming!" She introduced the first musician and the show began.

I willed myself not to look at Holliday. *Focus on the music,* I thought, staring at the stage. My strategy worked through the first two singer-songwriters. But near the end of the third performance—a guy with a big beard and a fast, angry song—I let my gaze drift.

Holliday was staring at me with her cold blue eyes.

Suddenly, everything felt uncomfortable. My dress felt scratchy. Aubrey's comb felt like a giant weight on my head. And Holliday's words clanged around my brain: *You're nothing special. I'm sure your music won't be, either.*

Her words echoed inside me while the girl with the cherry-colored hair was singing about her cheating ex-boyfriend, and after she finished and the audience clapped. They echoed as I picked up my guitar and stepped on the stage for my turn.

Onstage, the lights felt hot and bright, the way they had at the Ryman. This time, instead of feeling exhilarated, I felt seasick. I looked out into the audience. All I could see was darkness.

"I'm Tenney Grant," I said.

The mic zinged and I jumped, startled. I heard a supportive whoop that sounded like Mason. I shifted my guitar closer and plugged it in. Then I adjusted the microphone and started playing.

I was off from the moment I started. My tempo was too fast. Trying to slow down, I shifted my weight onto the other foot. That's when I dropped my pick. The guitar shuddered to a stop.

"Sorry," I mumbled. My face burned as I bent to pick it up.

Staycalmstaycalmstay—

"Okay," I said.

I started over. This time, I got through the intro and was just about to start singing the first verse, when I heard it. The A string was sharp. Suddenly, everything sounded wrong.

"Sorry," I said, and stopped again. I stood there, frozen, staring at the darkness beyond the edge of the stage.

Had I just ruined the biggest opportunity of my life?

FEELING THE HEAT

Chapter 17

*U*nder the stage lights, my skin felt like it was on fire. I stared at the stars clustered on my guitar frets, begging them for help. Somewhere in the audience, someone let out a concerned murmur. I squeezed my eyes shut, hoping that when I opened them I'd be back in my bedroom and this would all be a dream. As I did, though, I heard Mom's voice telling me, *Just be yourself.*

Something in me clicked. Maybe I'd messed up *part* of the most important performance of my life. But it wasn't over yet.

"Sorry, folks—technical problems," I said, retuning my A string. A few people laughed.

I noticed a chair tucked into a corner of the stage. I moved it to the microphone. I lowered the mic and sat on the chair cross-legged, shifting my guitar into my lap. Finally, I felt comfortable—I felt like myself.

I curled into my guitar and started the song over. After the intro, I glanced out at the audience. My eyes had adjusted and I could see people now, even Holliday. She suddenly seemed far away, and it no longer bothered me that she was there. All I wanted to do was sing.

"I am planted in the ground, tiny like a seed," I sang. *"Someday I will make you proud. I'll be steady like a tree. Will you teach me how to grow?"*

I glanced at my family. Mom was next to Dad, glowing with pride. With my eyes locked on hers, I poured my heart into the chorus.

"Gonna be myself, nobody else. Gonna reach the sky if I only try."

As I started the next verse, I heard my own voice for the first time since I'd stepped onstage. I sounded like my mother, my voice strong, clear, and unbroken. I played the chorus and then the bridge, my fingers dancing along the frets. I had played my song millions of times by now, but in this moment, I felt like I was hearing it anew.

FEELING THE HEAT

Every measure made me happy.

Finally, I played the last chords, lifting my fingers off the strings to make the ending pop. For a moment, I only heard silence. Then applause hit me in a crashing wave. Some people even gave me a standing ovation. Awe shivered through me. *They liked it!*

"Thank you so much," I said.

The moment the show finished, my family and Jaya swept me up in a wave of hugs.

"You were great!" said Aubrey.

"I love the changes you made to the second verse!" Mason said.

"I wish I hadn't messed up at the top," I said.

"It's not how you start, it's how you finish," Mom said, and Jaya nodded. I hoped they were right.

I looked around. "I'll be right back," I told Mom. "I want to find Portia."

I slipped through the crowd, craning my neck. When I finally found her, she was talking to the girl with the cherry-red hair.

"It was such an honor to meet you," the girl

said, shaking Portia's hand.

"My pleasure," said Portia, looking a little uncomfortable. She spotted me and gave me a wink.

I grinned, but before I could join their conversation, I felt a hand touch my elbow. I turned to find Holliday's mother beaming at me. Holliday stood behind her, grimacing like she'd just swallowed a lemon.

"Tenney, you were wonderful!" Mrs. Hayes gushed. "So much *talent!*"

"Thank you," I said.

"I know a future star when I see one, and you are *it*," she said. Then she turned to her daughter. "Holliday, maybe if you hadn't quit practicing, *you* could've been up on that stage with Tenney."

Holliday turned bright red.

"Holliday's wanted to be a country music starlet since she was seven," continued Mrs. Hayes, "but she hated playing guitar, and voice lessons didn't go so well."

"Mom!" Holliday hissed.

"It's fine, hon. You can't help it if you're tone deaf," Mrs. Hayes said, patting her on the shoulder.

Holliday stared at the ground, looking as if she wanted to disappear.

Suddenly, I felt bad for her. "Holliday's really good at other things," I said to Mrs. Hayes. I looked at Holliday. "Like planning! You're doing a great job on the Jamboree."

Holliday squinted at me, as if she couldn't figure out why I was being so nice.

"Thanks," she mumbled at last.

I excused myself and made my way back to our table, where Zane was talking to my parents.

"Tenney!" he said, noticing me. "Great song."

"Thank you," I said. My heart was hammering a mile a minute in my chest.

"I enjoyed your performance very much," Zane said. "I have to shake some hands, but I'd like to sit down later to discuss it with you and your parents. Is that all right?"

It was more than all right. This was the moment I had been waiting for.

Mason took Jaya and Aubrey home while my parents and I went to meet Zane at a nearby diner. The whole way there, I felt like I couldn't catch my breath. Even once my parents and I sat down in the booth across from Zane, it seemed like a fuzzy dream. I couldn't quite believe I was here, getting ready to talk with Zane Cale about *signing* to Mockingbird Records! After all, why would he have asked to meet in person if he *wasn't* going to sign me?

"Thank you for coming," Zane said, sipping his coffee.

"No, thank you," I said. "I'm really excited to be here."

I glanced up at my mom. *What if Zane offers to sign me and she says no?* I wondered. But my worries floated away when Mom squeezed my hand under the table.

Zane rocked back and forth thoughtfully. "Tenney, what happened at the beginning of your performance?" he asked, cocking his head.

Mom and Dad both bristled. Dad started to say something, but Zane Cale put up his hand.

"I'm asking Tenney," he said gently.

"Um, I was nervous. And I didn't feel like myself," I said.

Zane Cale nodded, watching me. His eyes were like a bloodhound's: soft and droopy, wise and maybe a little sad. "You know, I've been in music a long time, and I've found that the quickest way to fail as a performer is to *not* be yourself," he said. "You have to be authentic in everything you do, always. That's true in life, too, but it's especially true onstage. If you do something that isn't you, your audience can smell it."

"I agree," I said. I liked that he wasn't talking down to me.

"What do you like about writing music, Tenney?" he asked.

I thought for a second. "I like finding the right words to express how I feel," I said, "and I like performing my own songs."

"And why do you like to perform?" Zane asked.

"Because I want to say something with my music that people can relate to," I said.

Zane Cale nodded again. He nodded for so long that I wondered whether I'd said something wrong.

"I think you're extremely talented, as both
a songwriter and a performer, Tenney," he said
finally. "You have a fantastic voice and strong stage
presence. But you're also very young, which may be
why you got flustered onstage."

"Tenney's performed quite a bit with our family
band," Dad said.

Zane nodded, his eyes still locked on mine.
He leaned in. "Tenney, you were very good. But
I needed to see you own the stage the *whole* time
you're on it," he said sincerely. "I don't think you're
ready for a record contract."

"Oh," I said with a trembling voice.

We sat there in silence for a long moment. I
kept waiting for Zane to say something else, but he
didn't. I couldn't look at him, so I looked at Mom
instead. Her eyes were blazing.

"You could have told us this at the Bluebird,"
she said, "and spared Tenney's feelings."

Zane looked mystified. He shifted his gaze
over to me.

"Tenney, you want to have a career in music.
Right?"

FEELING THE HEAT

"Yes," I said.

"Ellie asked me to listen to you and think about your potential, so I did. I wanted to sit down with you face-to-face, to let you know my thoughts. The best thing for anyone in this business is to hear an honest opinion," he continued. "I think you have the potential to be a professional musician, Tenney. But I don't think you're ready. Not yet. Do you understand?"

I nodded. Hearing that made me feel a little better. "Thank you for taking the time to talk to me, Mr. Cale," I said, sitting up a little straighter.

"You're welcome," Zane Cale said, and he winked at me with one of his bloodhound eyes.

The drive home was one long, sad pause interrupted by my parents' attempts to make me feel better.

"It sounds like a record contract isn't even something Mockingbird would consider for someone your age," Dad said.

"Right," Mom agreed.

They both kept talking about what a good job I'd done. Finally, I told them I was over it, but I'm pretty sure they could tell I wasn't.

Mason was waiting for us out front when we got home. He started to ask what happened, but Mom hushed him. Watching Mason's expression change from excitement to pity made me feel even worse.

"I'm really tired," I said. "I'm going upstairs."

Aubrey was asleep in our room, but Waylon was by the foot of my bed, waiting for me. In the half-dark, I sat down and hugged him, letting myself feel devastated.

When I stepped into the hallway to go brush my teeth, I saw Mom. She was standing in the doorway to her room.

"Hey," she said softly. "Are you okay?"

I shrugged, feeling my bottom lip tremble with an uncried sob. "I know I shouldn't feel bad," I said, "but I feel like I failed."

"You didn't," Mom said firmly. "You were very brave to sit up on that stage all alone. And you were so good, honey." She hugged me, and I realized I'd never needed a hug so badly. Tears spilled down my cheeks as I tightened my arms around her.

"You can still play music, no matter what," Mom said. "That's the most important thing—to keep trying."

I knew she was right, but at that moment, my heart hurt too much to imagine ever playing again.

A NEW DEBUT

Chapter 18

*O*ver the next week, my family tiptoed around me. Mom made me even more blueberry muffins, and Dad gave me a new pick. Aubrey kept telling me how pretty I looked. It was like I'd been struck by lightning or something, and everyone was afraid they'd get shocked if they got too close. I knew they were trying to make me feel better, but it made me self-conscious.

To keep my mind off the showcase, I focused on homework and preparing with the Jamboree committee after school. I helped build stalls and painted banners and tied up straw bales that we would use for seating. Inside my head, I wasn't hearing music or thinking about lyrics, as I usually did—everything was silent. I didn't feel like myself, and I *really* didn't feel like performing. The problem was, I was still signed up for the Jamboree.

Finally, I told Ms. Carter I didn't think I wanted to perform anymore.

"Are you sure?" she asked, frowning.

I *wasn't* completely sure, but I nodded anyway.

"Okay," she said. "I'll find someone else to take your spot."

The morning of the Jamboree, some parents helped us bring everything over from the school gym to the senior center. The Jamboree committee spread out and started setting up the booths. I was fastening colorful fall leaves to some windows when I heard my name. I looked over. Portia was walking toward me, leaning on her walking stick.

"There you are!" she said. "I've been looking all over for you. We never really got to talk after your show at the Bluebird."

"Oh, right," I said. The showcase felt like it happened years ago.

"You were really good, once you found your

groove," Portia said. "The song was every bit as good as I remembered, too. I'm glad you took my advice about that bridge."

"Thanks," I said.

"Zane told me that you were pretty disappointed that he didn't sign you—" Portia paused and waited for me to respond, but I just stared at the ground to signal that I didn't want to talk about it. She seemed to understand and changed the subject.

"So! Have you been practicing for this shindig?" Portia asked, waving a hand at the corner of the yard where some parents were building the Jamboree stage.

I shook my head. "I'm not going to play today, actually," I said, feeling a twinge of regret.

Portia looked at me like I'd just told her I was moving to Mars.

Before she could say anything, I continued, "I told Ms. Carter to give my slot to someone who really wants to perform."

Portia's mouth twisted into a lopsided grimace. I thought she was going to try to convince me to play. Instead, she gave a tiny nod.

"Very well," she said. After a moment of awkward silence she said, "Can you excuse me for a minute? I need to say hi to someone."

Glad to be done with the uncomfortable questions, I went looking for Jaya. The courtyard swirled with activity. Game, food, and craft stalls had been set up on all sides around the Jamboree stage. A pink stall by one wall invited guests to MAKE YOUR OWN SWEET TEA! and catty-corner from that, the bake sale table stretched out forever, loaded with goodies. Papier-mâché trees with tissue-paper flowers curved around the doors to the courtyard like a garden arbor. Glittery strings of lights hung from a main tent pole, creating a magical, sparkly canopy. Surrounded by all this excitement, it was very hard to stay in a bad mood. Working on the Jamboree had made me feel part of something bigger than myself. Now, watching it unfold around me, I was flooded with pride for my school and my community.

I spotted Jaya setting up a corner stall with Frank. They were wearing rainbow-striped aprons and were surrounded by stacks of colored paper and a shiny metal printing press. As I walked up, Jaya lifted a colorful Jamboree poster off the press and clipped it to a clothesline above her to dry.

"Great poster!" I said, excited.

"Thanks!" Jaya said. "Want to see how we do it?"

Jaya showed me how to roll the ink onto the carved wooden letters in the press. Then she gently laid a piece of poster paper over the letters and slid a bar over it to press the paper into the ink. By the time my poster was dry, the Jamboree doors had opened and people were streaming in.

I spotted my family and waved them over.

Aubrey was practically squirming with excite-ment. "They have face painting! And a bouncy castle!" she cried, yanking Dad and Mason ahead.

Mom laughed and put her arm around me. "Do you want to introduce me to this Portia that I've been hearing all about?"

I brought Mom over to the bake sale table, but I didn't see Portia among the other volunteers.

"What a nice stage," Mom said, gesturing ahead of us to the wide circular platform. "It's

A NEW DEBUT

too bad you decided not to play."

"Yeah," I said, my eyes lingering on the stage. After a moment I spotted Ms. Carter and Portia stepping out from behind a tall speaker.

I grabbed Mom's arm and brought her over.

"Hey, I thought you were going to meet me at the baked goods table," I said as we approached.

"I had a different idea," Portia said, and shifted. I noticed that her guitar was slung across her back.

"Are you playing?" I said, surprised.

She nodded. "I thought I'd do a few songs," she said.

Mom was staring at Portia with a strange look on her face. I realized I'd forgotten to intro-duce them.

"Mom, this is my senior partner, Portia," I said.

"Yes, wow!" Mom said, her face turning red. She seemed all fluttery—and very un-Mom. "I'm a huge fan of your music, Ms. Burns."

I wrinkled my nose, confused. "What do you mean, a *fan*?" I asked.

"This is *Patty* Burns, honey," Mom said. "She's an amazing performer and songwriter."

I shook my head. "No, Mom. Her name is *Portia*."

Portia laughed. "My friends call me Portia. But my stage name is Patty."

My mom grabbed Portia's hands. "I saw you play the Ryman when I was eighteen. I remember it like it was yesterday!"

"So do I," Portia said, chuckling.

"Wait—you've played the *Ryman*?" I said, stunned.

"A couple of times," Portia said.

"Honey, she wrote 'April Springs,'" Mom said to me.

"No *way*," I said, realizing that this *whole* time I had been hanging out with the woman who wrote my favorite song. I blushed, suddenly remembering that I'd told Portia she needed to practice guitar more.

"Why didn't you tell me who you were?" I asked.

Portia waved a hand. "It wasn't important," she said. "But I'm glad you know now, so I can finally thank you."

I looked up, surprised. "Thank me? For what?"

"Without you, I'd still be sitting in a corner feeling sorry for myself," she said. "You helped me remember why I love music."

"I did?" I said, feeling my cheeks burn red.

"Yes, ma'am," Portia replied. "You're the first person I've met in a long time who loves music as much as me. That's why I told Ms. Carter I'd take your spot when you said you weren't going to perform—" She paused and gave me a coy smile. "And why I'm hoping you'll do me a favor and help me out onstage."

It took a second for me to really understand what she'd just said.

"Help *you* out—now?"

"Well, in about twenty minutes," Portia said with a chuckle. "Ms. Carter said you don't have to work the baked goods if you get up there with me. That is, if it's okay with your mom."

"It's up to Tenney," Mom replied, her eyes bright with pride.

"What do you say?" Portia asked me.

"Yes," I said. I felt like I could crack open from happiness.

"You should sing a Belle Starr song!" Aubrey
declared, on her tiptoes behind Mom. I was supposed to go on with Portia in just a few minutes, so
Mom was helping me get ready in the ladies' room.

"I think we've all heard enough Belle Starr
for one lifetime," Mom joked. She twisted my hair
back on one side, secured it with a bobby pin and
stepped back. "What do you think?" she asked.

I turned to the mirror. My hair looked simple
but pretty. I realized I was wearing the same outfit
I'd worn to the showcase, but this time, I didn't feel
so uncomfortable. Knowing that Portia would be
next to me onstage, I suddenly realized that I wasn't
as nervous as I had been before the showcase.

Portia was waiting for me by the stage with
Dad and Mason, who'd run home to get my guitar.
As we tuned our guitars side by side, I scanned the
lawn. The Jamboree had grown crowded. A large
crowd applauded the folk band that played before
us as they exited the stage.

"You ready, Tenney?" Portia asked.

I nodded. I felt a little buzzy, but I couldn't stop smiling as Ms. Carter stepped onstage and thanked everyone for coming to the Jamboree.

"We're so fortunate that a living music legend has agreed to close out the show today," she said, nodding to Portia. "She also has a last-minute guest: one of our most talented students, Tenney Grant!"

The audience started applauding as soon as Portia and I walked onstage.

"Hold on now!" she said into the microphone. "We haven't even started playing yet." The audience laughed.

"I'm going to let Tenney start this off." She winked at me and stepped back.

I moved to the microphone. A sea of faces smiled back at me in the sunlight. Just like that, happiness wrapped around me. "I'm Tenney Grant," I said, "and this one's for my mom."

I inhaled and took off, my fingers flying along the guitar frets and across the strings, picking out the intro.

"I am planted in the ground," I started, *"tiny like a seed..."*

My heart felt like it was floating. Rather than letting myself get lost in the song as I usually did when I was nervous, I looked out at the crowd. I knew my song so well by now that I could focus on connecting with the audience. They swayed to my song and clapped to the beat. By the last round of the chorus, they were singing along!

The moment I played the last chords, the crowd broke into applause.

"Thank you," I said into the microphone. "Now, I'd like to introduce Miss Patty Burns!"

The audience cheered as Portia stepped up to the mic. "I'm going to ask Tenney to sing this first one with me," she said.

I looked to Portia, surprised. We hadn't even rehearsed anything—how was I going to sing along if I didn't even know what we were playing?

She tossed me a reassuring grin and started playing. From the very first notes, I knew what song it was. As I joined in, our guitar lines blended together into my favorite song, "April Springs."

A NEW DEBUT

"*Last April the rains came down,*" sang Portia, "*And washed away your love.*"

I joined in with the harmony. "*Last April the rains came down, and washed away my pride. When I lost your heart in that rainstorm, I think I nearly died.*"

As our voices swirled in unison, people in the audience started singing along. I looked out at the crowd and glimpsed Mom and Dad beaming back at me. I let myself soar with the music. When the song ended, the crowd broke into a roar.

"Not too shabby," Portia whispered to me, and we took a bow together.

JUST THE BEGINNING

Chapter 19

J woke up on Monday feeling like I'd slept for a hundred years. Now that the Jamboree was over, it was easy to relax. I grinned all through breakfast and the drive to school, thinking about my performance.

I can't wait for the next time I get to perform, I thought, gliding down the hall to my locker. *Maybe I should ask Portia if she wants to play together again . . . ?*

Giggly whispers bubbled up behind me. Across the hall, a cluster of eighth-grade girls stared at me over their binders, twittering. The second they saw me looking, they shut up. Were they talking about me? My back stiffened and I opened my locker, trying to pretend I didn't see them. A tall girl with curly blonde hair walked over.

"Excuse me?" she said.

I turned, hugging my textbook like a shield. "Yes?"

"I thought you were awesome at the Jamboree," she said, her voice high with excitement. "Your song was amazing."

I felt color race to my cheeks. "Wow, thanks," I said.

The other girls came over.

"Where can I buy your songs?" one asked me. "Are they online?"

"When are you performing next?" questioned another.

"Um, I'm not sure," I said, scrambling. "And I haven't actually recorded any of my songs yet."

"*Yet*," said the tall redhead, grinning.

"I love 'Reach the Sky,'" she continued. "I watched the video like a thousand times yesterday! I even know all the words!"

The other girls nodded and all started talking at once.

I blushed with pride, but then caught myself. "Wait—what video?" I asked confused.

"The one from the Jamboree," the redhead replied. "It's online. You haven't seen it?"

I shook my head, dazed.

"You have to watch the video," piped up a girl with braids. "Everybody's talking about it!"

The next few minutes were a blur. I raced to Ms. Carter's room and found Jaya at her desk. She hadn't seen the video, either, but we had a few minutes until class started, so we got permission to use the classroom computer.

"Search under Tenney Grant and Magnolia Hills Jamboree," Jaya said as I typed.

The video popped up as a tiny freeze-frame of me onstage with my guitar. "Here it is!" I said.

Jaya leaned over my shoulder, reading the caption. "Music's next superstar, onstage with rock-country legend Patty Burns."

I clicked on the video link. The recording started with me singing "Reach the Sky." It was sort of blurry, but the audio was good.

"Tenney!" Jaya exclaimed. "Look how many people have watched it!"

My breath caught when I saw the view count—

JUST THE BEGINNING

more than 10,000 people had viewed my video!

We scrolled down to read the comments.

"This person said you have an amazing voice!" Jaya said, pointing to the screen. "This one says, *I can't wait to buy her album. When's it coming out?*"

"This is crazy!"

"No," Jaya proclaimed, bouncing in her chair. "*This* is just the beginning."

For the rest of the day, I did my best to concentrate on my classes. But the minute school got out, I raced out to the school's front steps. As usual, Mason was waiting for me by the flagpole.

"Mason, do you have your phone with you?" I asked breathlessly. I told him about the video, and he immediately got out his phone to check the site.

"Holy cow," he said, looking down at the screen. "Tenney, you're up to 15,000 views!"

We hurried through the Five Points intersection to Dad's music store. I was about to rush in to tell Dad about the video, but froze when I looked through the front window. Inside, Zane Cale was talking to Dad by the cash register.

"What's he doing here?" Mason said, frowning over my shoulder.

"No idea," I said.

We walked in. Zane tipped his porkpie hat to me like an old-fashioned gentleman.

"Hi, Zane," I said, trying to act cool.

"Tenney," he replied.

"Mr. Cale stopped by to talk to you," Dad said. His eyes sparkled with excitement.

"I wanted to tell you how great you were at the Jamboree," Zane said.

"I—I didn't know you were there," I said, flustered.

"I was indeed," Zane said. "I've known Portia Burns for a long time. When she called me that morning saying she was going to play her first show since her stroke, I came to support her. Seeing you was an unexpected bonus." He looked me straight in the eye. "Last time we talked, you made it very clear that it's important to you to be true to yourself. And this time around I saw it. You completely commanded the stage and connected with your audience in a way I hadn't seen at the showcase. You had a passion and a fire that blew my boots off."

"Thank you," I said.

"When I saw you on that Jamboree stage, I realized it's only a matter of time before someone else in the music business sees it, too. So I thought before that happened, I needed to make a deal with you."

Boom. Just like that, my heart felt like it stopped.

"I can't offer you a record contract right now," he continued, "because I still think you need time to mature as an artist. From time to time, however, I help develop songwriters. I provide advice, help them book performances, and give guidance on their music. Then when they're ready, I produce their album. I'd like to do that for you, as your manager. That is, if you're interested," he said to me.

Mason frowned, crossing his arms.

"Funny how you didn't want to sign Tenney until her video went viral," he said.

"What video?" Dad asked. Zane looked just as perplexed.

Mason showed them the video on his phone. "19,000 views!" he whispered to me.

"Well, that is an accomplishment," Zane said.

"But that's not why I'm here. I don't work with people based on viral videos. I work with them because I believe in them. I'm not interested in turning you into the next Belle Starr. You shouldn't try to be anyone other than Tenney Grant. Your music needs to reflect who you are. That's something that takes time to grow and develop, but it's the only way to build a long-lasting career." He replaced his hat on his head and looked me dead in the eye. "So, what do you think? Will you work with me?"

I hesitated. I liked Zane, and I felt in my bones that he meant what he said about helping me grow as an artist. But I remembered what had happened to Mom. She'd trusted someone in the music business . . . and he'd stolen her songs.

"I need to think about it," I said.

After dinner, Aubrey sat at the computer in the corner of the kitchen, tracking the number of video views. "21,341!" she announced.

Mason rinsed a plate and handed it to me to

JUST THE BEGINNING

put into the dishwasher. "I can't believe that you told Zane you'd have to think about it!" he said.

"It's a big decision," I told him, glancing at Mom.

She hadn't said much all night. Was she just trying to figure out how to tell me that I couldn't work with Zane? I thought about how she had lost all her songs without even knowing it was happening. *That would break my heart*, I realized. *If she tells me I have to turn Zane down, I know it's because she doesn't want me to get hurt.*

Even so, I couldn't bear the thought of saying no to Zane. For just a little longer, I needed to enjoy the excitement of Zane's offer and all the possibilities it carried.

"I'm going to get some air," I said.

I got my guitar and my songwriting journal and sat out on the porch with Waylon. At first I couldn't focus with Aubrey calling out the number of views for my video every ten seconds. After a while, her voice blended with the crickets into a strange kind of music.

I paged through my journal. In the front were

the first songs I'd written when I was ten: the one about Waylon, and another about Christmas. Although they were simple, I'd spent a lot of pages working on the rhymes and changing the lyrics until I found what worked best. As I got older, I wrote longer songs and learned to choose my words more carefully. By the time I got to the page where I'd worked out the lyrics for "Reach the Sky," I could see how far I'd come. Still, I knew I had a long way to go.

The porch creaked behind me. I looked up to see Mom stepping out from the kitchen.

"Hey," she said, sitting down next to me.

"Hi." I took a deep breath.

"Are you okay?" she asked.

"I'm not sure," I said, sighing. "I want to work with Zane, but I'm afraid that you're going to say no. But I get it: You worked with that producer guy and it turned out to be awful . . ." I trailed off.

"Tenney," Mom said, taking my hand, "this isn't about my past. This is about your future. Dad and I would never let anybody take advantage of you and your music. The most important thing to us is that you feel good about yourself and that you never give up your love of music."

She paused, her eyes wet with tears. I steadied myself, prepared for disappointment.

She continued, "If you decide you want to work with Zane, your dad and I promise to support you."

I drew in a sharp breath. "You mean, this is *my* decision?"

Mom smiled. "Yes, it is. But if there's ever a time that you don't like the direction he's going with your music, you can stop. You will always have that choice—your dad and I will make sure of that. Okay?"

I nodded, and threw my arms around her. Her hug made me feel totally safe. I knew I could tell her anything. "But what if I try and try and Zane decides I'm not good enough?"

"Good enough for what?" Mom asked.

"To make an album," I said.

"So what?" Mom said. "As long as you believe in yourself, you can keep making music. If making music is something you really want to do, you don't run away from it. You say yes to it. And you know that no matter what happens, we're proud of you. Right?"

"Right," I said, letting out a deep breath. "Thank you, Mom."

Mom kissed my head and went back inside.

I looked up at twinkling stars in the darkening sky. I felt like one of those stars, floating higher than I could ever imagine, shining with my whole heart.

Remember this feeling, I thought to myself. *It'll make a great song.*

SONG LYRICS

Reach the Sky

by Leah Bryan and Hannah Fisher

I am planted in the ground
Tiny like a seed
Someday I will make you proud
I'll be steady like a tree
Will you teach me how to grow?

Chorus:
Gonna be myself, nobody else
Gonna reach the sky if I only try

I admit that I am young
Tucked beneath your wings
But someday I'll be on my own
Wild and flying free
Will you teach me how to sing?

Gonna be myself, nobody else
Gonna reach the sky if I only try

Bridge:
I know you wanna keep me
Safe away at home
But I've got my own dreams
And I can't tell them no

Gonna be myself, nobody else
Gonna reach the sky if I only try

ABOUT THE SONGWRITERS

Growing up just outside Nashville, sisters Leah Bryan and Hannah Fisher were surrounded by great music and talented singer-songwriters. Like Tenney, they were born into a musical family that performed together at community events.

Their big break came in 2000 when the Peasall Sisters—Leah, Hannah, and their sister Sarah—were invited to record songs for the soundtrack of the film *O Brother, Where Art Thou?* The album was a huge hit, and at the ages of eight and eleven, Leah and Hannah became the youngest people ever to win a Grammy. Riding a wave of success, the family of eight set off on a ten-year tour across the country. "It was fun and we loved it," says Hannah, looking back on the tour. "But it was definitely hard work."

Now in their twenties, they still enjoy performing with their family. They claim that they've been playing together for so long that they can just give each other a look and know what they're going to play next.

Leah and Hannah sing "Reach the Sky" at the Bluebird Cafe in Nashville.

This sense of family connectedness was very important as Leah and Hannah cowrote "Reach the Sky" while living five hundred miles apart from each other! Communicating by text message, they patched the song together by sending lyrics and sound clips of the melody.

Inspired by Tenney's story and their own experiences as young musicians, the sisters wrote about the importance of staying true to oneself. Leah offers this advice to young songwriters like Tenney: "There's nobody like you. Be yourself and don't worry about the rest. Great music will always find its way out there—just not always in the ways you might think."

SPECIAL THANKS

With gratitude to manuscript consultant
Erika Wollam Nichols for her insights and
knowledge of Nashville's music industry; to
music director Denise Stiff for guiding song
development; to songwriters Hannah Fisher
and Leah Bryan for helping Tenney find her
voice; and to Taylor Guitars for giving Tenney
the guitar of her dreams.

ABOUT THE AUTHOR

As a young reader, Kellen Hertz loved L. Frank Baum's Wizard of Oz series. But since the job of Princess of Oz was already taken, she decided to become an author. Alas, her unfinished first novel was lost in a sea of library books on the floor of her room, forcing her to seek other employment. Since then Kellen has worked as a screenwriter, television producer, bookseller, and congressional staffer. She made her triumphant return to novel writing when she coauthored *Lea and Camila* with Lisa Yee before diving into the Tenney series for American Girl.

Kellen lives with her husband and
their son in Los Angeles.

Request a FREE catalogue at
americangirl.com/catalogue

Sign up at **americangirl.com/email**
to receive the latest news and exclusive offers

READY FOR AN ENCORE?

VISIT

americangirl.com

for Tenney's world

OF BOOKS, APPS, GAMES, **QUIZZES**, *activities,* AND MORE!